MAX'S CAMPERVA]

CAMPFIRES
AND
Dead Liars

TYLER RHODES

Copyright © 2025 Tyler Rhodes

All rights reserved. This book or any portion thereof may not be reproduced or used in any manner whatsoever without the express written permission of the author except for the use of brief quotations in a book review.

This is a work of fiction. Names, characters, businesses, places, events and incidents are either the products of the author's imagination or used in a fictitious manner. Any resemblance to actual persons, living or dead, or actual events is purely coincidental.

Dedicated to all the fire starters.

Chapter 1

"That's us paid for a few nights, Anxious." I settled in the driver's seat and smiled at my best buddy, sitting upright beside me, eyes twinkling with excitement because we were somewhere new.

I buckled up, and drove away from the entrance to Shell Island, then pulled into a parking spot so we could have a quick chat about our plans.

Anxious cocked his head and whined a question, so I figured it was only fair to fill him in on my thoughts.

"According to the woman I just paid, the island is huge, but not quite an island. Yes, I know it's confusing. It's the largest campsite in the UK, possibly Europe, but is only called an island because some days it gets cut off by the tidal estuary for a few hours. Quite a few beauty spots in West and North Wales are by estuaries. Remember Barmouth, and Aberdyfi?"

Anxious barked in the affirmative. We'd had some great times at both locations, and we'd even stayed just a stone's throw from Shell Island at Harlech, with its amazing castle and stunning beaches. We'd also had a rather gruesome murder mystery to solve in the area, so it felt like returning to the scene of the crime, even though it wasn't us who'd committed the foul deed.

"What she also told me is that we can pick a pitch wherever we like! No limit to what space you take up here. Brilliant, eh?"

The cutest Jack Russell Terrier both sides of the Wales/England border yawned.

I chuckled as I said, "Not so impressed? It's unusual, as most campsites are starting to charge for every possible extra. Lots make you pay for dogs, gazebos, extra tents, and it becomes expensive. So this is great. We can spread out and go anywhere. The place is so big, though, that I'm not sure where to go. We have the beach side with the sand dunes, which might be nice as we can hunker down out of the wind, although it's really still today and super sunny, or we can go over to the harbour side, where we can watch boats, and apparently it's good for crabbing. You like crabbing, don't you?"

An ear-splitting bark was all the answer I needed.

"Then it's settled. We'll find a pitch close to the sand dunes, then walk over to the harbour for some crabbing. Do you still have your bucket and the line?" I asked, sniggering.

The wise little guy hissed through sparkling white teeth, telling me it wasn't nice to make fun of him because of the last time we'd tried catching crabs.

"Sorry, I was only joking. I couldn't help remembering what happened. Don't let them get you with their pincers."

Anxious held up a paw and whimpered, reminding me that it was at the castle where he'd sustained an injury to his paw. He'd been milking it ever since, trying it on with new friends to get some sympathy and hopefully a treat.

"I know you hurt it, but it's better now. Come on, let's have a drive around and see what we like the look of."

Vee spluttered into life, then purred loudly, a throaty belch interrupting the mellow rumble I'd grown to adore over almost a year of living in my beloved 67 VW Campervan. My home on wheels was so much more than merely a place to rest my head and a means of getting from one place to another. She was part of me now, and I knew every square inch of the interior. Space was so important that I must have re-arranged my belongings literally hundreds of times as my vanlife progressed and I slowly eased into this peculiar but incredibly rewarding way of life.

Sometimes I felt like a crab, and the van was my shell. A hermit crab who never wanted to change its home. I adored it. The slightly too small rock n roll bed, the hassle of having to pull it out every night, leaving me with almost zero room to move. Tidying it away back to a bench seat every morning and sorting out the bedding was an inescapable routine, and routine was important, maybe even more so than when living in a house. Something to ground me, something familiar, and something strangely comforting. But most important of all was that Vee gave me the freedom to go where I wanted, sleep wherever I parked, and afforded access to the great outdoors. That was the true beauty of this nomadic lifestyle I had chosen to lead. An almost free pass to the wonders of the British countryside. Beaches, small towns, quaint villages tucked away amongst rolling hills, back-to-basics campsites or large operations like here at Shell Island. The diversity and the ability to move on whenever I chose was freeing in a way it was impossible to describe unless you'd sampled this life for yourself.

Shell Island was a revelation. I knew it was huge, but not how impressive it turned out to be. I'd heard talk about it being difficult to pick a spot, and many ended up driving around and around the various small roads, unable to decide where to make camp, and as it turned out they were entirely correct. Whereas usually I would arrive at a campsite and either be given a pitch or allowed to choose, the options were always very limited, as most sites were a field or two at most. Here, there were endless fields, little hidden spots down dead-end roads, or acres exposed to the sun and wind. You could camp in the sand dunes, right by the beaches, pick a high spot with views out across the water, go into what appeared to be a party field where large groups of people were already on the beers, or right by the side of the roads—the choice was endless.

I was struck with indecision. Too much choice left me fretting about not picking the right spot, making it more complicated than it should have been.

After driving around the massive site for the second time, I turned to Anxious and said, "Right, that's it. We'll take the next road down towards the sand dunes and park. Otherwise, we'll be driving around all day and miss out on this fantastic weather. I'm hungry too. It will be lunchtime soon."

Anxious barked his agreement, so with a nod I took a left turn, trundled down a potholed sandy track, then we both gasped as we glanced off to the right.

"Look at that! It's perfect."

We grinned at each other, so I drove off the track onto the scrubby ground, not quite sand, not quite earth either, then pulled on the handbrake and turned off the engine. Vee ticked pleasantly, as pleased as us to finally take a breather.

With Anxious' seatbelt unclipped, I released my own then got out. The little guy hopped down and we stood for a moment, breathing deeply of the salty air, and lifted our faces to the sun.

"Can you feel that, buddy? That's freedom. You can't put a price on it, but wow, is this place awesome or what?"

Anxious wandered off and cocked a leg on a patch of hardy grass. Clearly, he wasn't feeling as poetic as me.

I inspected the fantastic spot I'd chosen, pleased with my choice. The view was open to the west towards the water just visible between towering sand dunes. Behind us, and on either side, the dunes rose, giving us protection from the wind and the sounds of other visitors, making it feel like we had the whole island to ourselves. Tucked away down here, we could have been the only souls around, yet just a few minutes away was the large entrance that contained not only a shop and the visitor check in, but a pub and restaurant. This was a large-scale operation, but clearly well run and extremely popular. I loved it.

While Anxious explored, I set about making camp. With the side of Vee open, I erected my fancy gazebo right beside her, vowing not to leave for a few days so I got it as close as I could, meaning I could step from Vee into the shelter. I left the front unzipped for the view, but kept two walls closed so that's where I arranged my kitchen. With my setup streamlined, it didn't take long to unfold the large table, sort out the gas stove, stack the boxes with foodstuff and crockery, arrange everything how I liked it, then lay down the blanket so it felt lovely and cosy and like a massive van extension.

No cooking inside the cramped conditions for me. Everywhere I went lately people were doing the same thing. Many new van conversions had done away with sinks and cookers inside their vehicles, opting instead for pull-out drawers on the sides or rear, or used a table like me. It gave you tons more space and stopped the interior getting stinky and covered in grease. It was the way forward, a different approach to vanlife that made more sense, especially with the plethora of gazebos, awnings, or drive-away tents now available to double or triple your space for ten to twenty minutes of work erecting them.

Pleased with the local scents, content there were no rabbits mocking him from a distance, and satisfied no seagulls were about to attack, Anxious took one last glimpse at the sky to be sure, then with a huff settled on the rug and curled up.

"Tired already?" I asked, shaking my head.

He opened an eye, then closed it again. I had my answer.

Feeling content with my lot, and buoyed by the location and the beautiful sunshine, I retrieved my chair and settled at the entrance to the gazebo and sank low with a groan of pure contentment. This was the life.

With nothing left to do but enjoy my stay, my thoughts drifted back to the reason we'd come. I pulled the slip of paper from my shirt pocket and unfolded it. I must have read it a hundred times, turned it over, looked under different lights, but the message remained the same. Shell Island. That was all it said. Someone had put it there a few days ago at the cheese pie festival, but so far there was zero clue who that was, or why they'd wanted me to come. Min swore it wasn't her, and I believed her. So who?

I glanced back at Vee and the strange graffiti adorning the orange paintwork of the two-tone body, and wondered if it was related. Had whoever created the bizarre patchwork spray painting also left the message? What did it all mean? With my life seemingly consisting of one mystery after another, I wasn't unduly concerned, and felt no sense of danger or malice with either, but it was confounding and I hated not being able to solve the mysteries. Hopefully, all would reveal itself soon enough, so for now I vowed to leave it be and not stress about it. How could I when we were in such an incredible place?

Keen to explore on foot, yet enjoying merely sitting and soaking up the vibe, I remained where I was for a while, listening to the gulls, the waves lapping at the shore, faint voices in the distance of people having fun, and watched the occasional camper wander past through the dunes or along the dirt track. Someone on a quad drove past with stacks of firewood in nets, presumably making deliveries. I still had some, but it was good to know it was available to buy.

Not wanting to eat too early as it was still only eleven, I pushed down the hunger pangs and stood then called for Anxious. He was up like a shot and raring to go, so I locked Vee even though it felt unnecessary, grabbed my satchel, then checked myself in the wing mirror. Not out of vanity, but more as a way of reconnecting with what I actually looked like. It was easy to go days, sometimes weeks, without seeing my own reflection, leaving me feeling like a stranger when confronted with my own face.

The beard was still long, although quite straggly, but presentable enough. My tan was coming along nicely now I was back to wearing vests, cut-off faded denim jeans, and my trusty Crocs, making my blue eyes turn the familiar almost green. My hair hung partway down my back when wet, but the curls lifted it enough so it rested on my shoulders, the brown streaked with a hint of grey now, which I didn't mind. Not too shabby, if somewhat unkempt, but another sign of the freedom I felt, and no longer trying to conform and worry about what others thought of me.

Whistling a merry tune, I sauntered along the track, the dry ground morphing into sand the closer we got to the beach. Anxious darted off, so I trailed after him into the dunes, huffing and puffing up the narrow path and dodging tufts of local hardy grasses that somehow thrived in the salty air and the almost dead ground. How did they survive with so few nutrients? It was perplexing.

My mind elsewhere, I almost fell over a small tent nestled at the base of the dune, tucked away in an oasis of calm, entirely hidden from sight.

"Oi!" came a disgruntled cry from inside the tent as the guy rope pinged when I stepped away.

Anxious barked and looked around for signs of the man who'd shouted, then edged towards the one-man tent entrance, sniffing seriously, then yowled and jumped back, hackles raised as the zipper snapped around the doorway angrily and a tanned face popped out.

"Sorry about that. I didn't even notice the tent. Nice spot you have here."

"Sweet, eh?" beamed a slight figure of a man as he crawled out from his tent and I caught a glimpse of the chaos inside. How could he sleep inside with so much mess? How did he find the room to lie down?

"Um, yes, very, er, snug."

Brushing down a pair of faded black jeans, the man stood and stretched out his wiry frame, his bare arms tanned and his plain white tee rather stained. He grinned, one of his front teeth missing as he dragged a hand over his lined face. I guessed him to be mid-fifties, but he could have been a decade either way as it was clear he'd just woken up.

He glanced back at his tent and shook his curly hair, noting, "I left my van back by the track as I wanted to get right into the dunes. Bit cramped, and I brought too much stuff, but I had a roaring fire last night right on the beach. Tonight I'm going back to the campervan."

"I'm not far away in mine. A 67 VW."

"Sweet. I've got a brand new Transporter. Top of the range, fully kitted out. Has all the bells and whistles, but sometimes it's good to sleep on the ground, you know?"

"Sure. It's nice to mix things up. Did you get the conversion done or do it yourself?"

"I got a great local company to do the whole thing. Best spec you can get. Went for one of those double bench seat configurations where you can turn it into U seating with a table that you use to convert it into a full-size bed. Got a pull-out drawer at the rear with built-in sink and a cooker, tons of storage too. Lots of solar and a massive double battery pack and even a diesel heater. It's awesome!"

"Sounds incredible. Bet you love it, don't you?"

"Sure do. Been mine for a few months now. Before that I had an older model with a homemade conversion, which I did an awesome job of by the way, but it was time for a change. I earn good money doing local sightseeing trips and whatnot so figured why not? After all, it's my home."

"How long have you been a vanlifer?"

"Blimey, it's been ages. Years and years. Well over a decade. I lose track. I'm Ben, by the way." Ben scratched at his stubble, then frowned as Anxious pawed at his shins. "Oh, hey there, little fella."

"I'm Max, and that's Anxious."

"Aw, what's the matter, eh?" Ben squatted easily and rubbed Anxious' head, causing him to groan then roll over for a tummy tickle.

"It's his name, not his emotional state," I explained for the millionth time.

"Ah, okay." Ben frowned, then smiled as he stood and extended a hand.

We shook, then stood apart, taking the measure of each other for a moment but trying not to make it obvious.

Ben scratched his chin again, his eyes constantly roaming, glancing off to each side.

"Something wrong?"

"Eh? Um, no, just taking stock." Ben grinned, then his eyes widened as he looked past me.

I turned in time to see someone in full camouflage military garb storm towards us, a mean-looking rifle pointing at us, their face hidden by a balaclava.

"What the…" Before I could finish the sentence, the stranger spun the weapon expertly and smashed the stock into my forehead.

Just another day at the beach was my last thought before I sank into a very dark place.

Chapter 2

My entire world consisted of one thing.
Pain.
As I slowly came back to reality, I found it impossible to think. My head throbbed so deeply it was all-consuming. What had happened? Why did it hurt so bad? Lying on the ground, not daring to stand or even sit up, I lifted my arm and put a hand to my forehead. A golf ball-sized lump was my reward for such a foolish move, and touching it even as lightly as I had sent waves of pain shooting through my skull. Nausea rose until I gasped then blacked out.

When I resumed consciousness for the second time, I remembered exactly what had happened, which didn't make me feel any better at all. Still concussed, with my memory more shaky than my legs, I tried to stand but did nothing but cause myself more pain as I collapsed onto the prickly grass and got a mouthful of sand. Spitting it out, stuck on all fours, I felt like a sick dog. The moment I had that thought panic rose and I turned my head painfully, searching for Anxious.

Where was he? I tumbled over onto my side and attempted to call for him, but no words would come, just a hoarse whisper. Rather than force things, I remained motionless and let the waves of sickness and the intense pounding in my head engulf me, knowing it couldn't last forever, astounded how long it did continue for. Wave after wave of agony swirled in my skull like it was full of knives, piercing my nerves.

Would it never end? Would I ever feel normal again? When would I be able to move? To speak? To turn my head even?

Eventually, the sickness subsided and the pain became at least manageable, so I curled up, each movement sending new and ever more intense shooting pains through my skull, but I managed to get into a sitting position and take stock of things.

Ben's tent was directly in front of me, but there was no sign of him or Anxious. The attacker was gone too. Still reeling, and unsure if I was imagining things or I really had been assaulted, I could do nothing but wait it out until the fog in my mind cleared and I could begin to think straight. Had I taken a fall and dreamed of being hit with the rifle? Could that be what happened? It was impossible to think it through properly. Every time I tried, the agony engulfed me and I had no choice but to let the thoughts drift by as nothing would make sense.

It must have been minutes before I felt able to put the pieces together, but as soon as I did I panicked. Someone in full military gear, with a rifle no less, had stormed towards us, Ben had looked freaked out, Anxious hadn't even had time to react, neither had I, then they slammed the stock of the weapon into me and I'd fallen like a total dolt, not even trying to defend myself. It had all happened too fast, and was so unexpected, especially because it was so at odds with the beautiful surroundings.

A cough caught me unawares and caused a cascade of torturous barbs to blast my skull like someone was hammering at me from the inside with a pick. Sickness rose again and I closed my eyes and grimaced, praying for it to be over. As it subsided, I looked around, hoping to see Anxious, but he wasn't there. Not caring how much it would hurt, I steeled myself then called as loudly as I could for the little guy, wishing with all my heart that he'd come bounding towards me, tongue lolling, ears flapping, and tail wagging merrily.

He didn't.

I was alone.

I don't know what came over me, but for some reason I prodded my forehead again, the pain incredible, but it felt like the lump had gone down a little. Beginning to really panic now, as what if the man had taken Anxious, I clambered to my feet, regardless of how much it hurt, and stood on shaky legs as a terrible sickness slammed into me like a truck and I almost blacked out again. I fought it with everything I had, refused to give in as I had to find Anxious. The moment I got a grip on things I called for him. It was no use. My voice was hoarse and barely more than a whisper, so he wouldn't hear me if he'd got lost, although that would be very unlikely.

Thinking things through for a moment, I concluded that I had to take things one step at a time. First thing to do was to check the tent, so I staggered over, vision blurring more with every step, and I had to stop repeatedly until I'd covered the short distance. Back on all fours, I crawled into the tiny space that was rammed with Ben's gear. A sleeping bag, a roll of foam that was unused, a cheap nylon backpack stuffed with clothes, all of which stank and were clearly dirty, and scattered everywhere were boots, more clothes, several mystery books, a torch, two empty bottles of cheap wine, plastic cups, and a whole lot of nothing else. No wallet, no phone, no pieces of paper with an address or even Ben's full name, and where were the keys to his new van?

Finally thinking more clearly, I rummaged through everything again and shifted things around so I could search properly, then found a secret pocket on the side of the tent and inside was a key on a VW leather keyring. It was almost an antique, not like that for a new van, just a simple key rather than even a fob, so what was he doing with this for an old VW campervan rather than his new one? How perplexing. Nevertheless, I stuffed it into my pocket, went through the rucksack for the third time, searched everywhere again, even inside the boots and the sleeping bag, but came up empty-handed.

Sweating badly, sick beyond belief, and terribly thirsty, I backed out and lay there for a moment to cool down, but the sun was at its zenith now and fiercely strong. I knew I couldn't remain the way I was or heatstroke would be added to my already long list of woes.

With my senses reeling, my eyes watering, skull pounding, and a tight knot of utter dread threatening to overwhelm me, I did the only thing I could and simply put one foot in front of the other and walked. I saw nobody as I returned to Vee, and didn't even think about it or anything else. I had to use all my powers of concentration merely to remember how to perform a task as simple and ingrained as walking. The dunes were a test of my determination and willpower and I managed to get between them and take the path we'd used earlier as we headed towards the water, all thought of that now forgotten in my panic to find Anxious, get a drink, and find shade so I didn't collapse right here.

Vee took my breath away as I spied her across the track, and I staggered over, almost falling repeatedly, but made it into the glorious shade and grabbed for the sides of the gazebo to steady myself, gasping with relief as the cooler air enveloped me. I reached out with a shaking hand and took a bottle of water but dropped it because my fingers refused to function properly. Sighing, and prepared for the inevitable, I bent. Blood rushed to my head and I felt close to blacking out, but managed to snatch it and stand then waited for the wooziness to subside.

When I felt ready, I unscrewed the lid and chugged, unable to get enough to quench my thirst. With the bottle held tightly, and my legs about to give way, I lunged for the chair, managed to get hold of the arm, then eased into it with a cry of pain as Ben's key stabbed into my backside. I didn't care. No way was I going to stand up just yet.

"Where are you, Anxious?" I whispered, the loss gnawing at me, dread crawling up my spine.

What could have happened? Why were we

assaulted? Where was Ben? Had the attacker taken him? Stolen Anxious? Was my best buddy hurt? Or worse? It didn't bear thinking about.

There was nothing for it; I had to find him no matter what. Where to start? Better take a look at my noggin first. That would be the sensible thing to do. With my thoughts finally clear, and feeling recovered after the water and a brief stint in the shade, I heaved off the chair, tested my balance which was much improved, then walked carefully over to Vee and patted her, just for the feeling of companionship. She was warm, and it felt like home. It was home.

The sight I was confronted with in the wing mirror came as a shock. The lump was massive and already dark with the bruising, but there was no cut, so I didn't need stitches. I should probably see a doctor as I clearly had concussion, but if I was thinking straight then surely I was okay? Even if I wasn't, I couldn't leave without Anxious. I bent lower to check myself over better, and the key jabbed into me again.

It was like a lightbulb went off and I almost palm-slapped my forehead but caught myself in time—that wouldn't be a good idea. Chuckling, and shaking my head, which was also a terrible idea, I stood, got myself another bottle of water which I stuffed into my satchel, then carefully retraced my steps to Ben's tent, constantly on the lookout for any sign of either Anxious or Ben and whoever had assaulted me. I saw nothing, but got to the tent soon enough then searched around for footprints and found what I was looking for clearly in the sand heading between the dunes towards what I hoped would be Ben's van. Still confused about the old key rather than a new one for his modern Transporter, I followed the footprints as best I could, losing them a few times but finding them again after a little searching.

With my eyes glued to the ground, I literally walked straight into an ancient, battered VW Transporter that was parked in the dunes off a narrow track that I guessed hardly ever got used. Frowning, I stood back to get a proper look, noting the rust, the faded blue paint job from years of sun exposure, and the junk littering the dashboard. There were no other vehicles around, but surely this couldn't be Ben's? He said he had a new model, all kitted out, but that he used to have an old van before he bought the new one. I cupped my hands and peered through the windscreen, noting the piles of clothes and other junk scattered over the passenger seat and floor, but a curtain blocked the view to the back. I tried the side window, but again the curtain was drawn.

Shrugging, I figured I had nothing to lose, so tried the key in the door. It turned easily. What was going on here? Was Ben a liar? Had he made up a story about buying a new van? Why do that to a complete stranger? What was the point?

Confused, I nevertheless slid the door open. It was stiff, and wobbled on the runners which needed replacing, but I hauled on it and it clicked into place. It took a moment for my eyes to adjust to the gloom of the interior, but once they did I almost wished I hadn't been able to see. It was a vanlifer's worst nightmare, and I couldn't fathom how Ben could live like this.

The interior fit-out was a standard configuration with a rock n roll bed, which was in bench seat position, and a compact kitchen on the opposite side to me, with a floor-to-ceiling wardrobe to the right of the counter. Doors were hanging off their hinges. The MDF was in an embarrassing state with peeling paintwork, chunks missing, the edge banding hanging in strips like flayed skin. The sink was full of dirty dishes, the single ring hob was black with grease and covered with more dirty plates, and that was the good part.

The bench seat was swamped with clothes, blankets, a sleeping bag, and several coats, and what little floor space there was had a collection of boots, wellies, umbrellas, most of which was useless in the warm weather, and more piles of clothes and blankets. How could he live like this? Why had he lied to me? How did he move about in here? I guess this explained why Ben was camping. There was no room to sleep in here. Did the rock n roll bed even work? The leather was in tatters, and the smell inside was seriously funky, so what would it be like inside with the doors closed? Unbearable, that's what.

Standing right there with my head poked inside was too much for me. It wasn't my obsession with keeping things neat and tidy that made this seem so bad, was it? This was clearly someone with issues, right? This was no way to live. Was this really Ben's van? Maybe he'd just found a key. Maybe his was somewhere else. I had to be sure. After my initial inspection, I knew I had to look more closely, so took a deep breath then clambered inside, standing on filthy clothes and blankets. There was a bag in the corner, an old military green satchel like mine, but in poor condition.

Inside was a mean-looking knife, certainly not your every day carry kind, a battered hip flask, loose change, and in a pocket I found a wallet. A bank card with the name Ben Watson, and a driver's license card with his photo made me certain that this really was Ben's van. After a thorough search, and coming up with nothing else, I used the key and unlocked the front, then checked through the junk and the glove compartment, finding nothing of interest or help.

All that remained was to search the rear. It was the only way to look inside part of the wardrobe, and there might be things under the back seat or in the small garage area conversions like this usually had, so I hurried to the back and opened the door up, the shade welcome. I flung open the sole cupboard door nervously, sweating over what I'd find, worried a pile of unwashed clothes would tumble out onto my head.

"Anxious!"

My heart skipped a beat, my sickness and pain were forgotten, but then I almost collapsed with dread because before me on a blanket, tucked into the tiny cupboard amongst random tools and covered in a blue hoodie was the still form of my beloved best friend. I bent and scooped him up, dreading that he would feel cold and limp, but he was warm and his nose twitched as I stood erect and moved my head close to his. One eye opened, and he licked my nose, tail thumping against my arm.

"Have you been napping?" I laughed, beside myself with joy.

Anxious barked a negative, then licked my nose again.

"You were. You were sleeping. Are you alright? Did the man hurt you? You're boiling hot. You must be so thirsty. Who would lock a dog in a van in this heat? You poor thing."

Anxious shook in my arms, clearly still groggy from his doze, but came around properly and began to squirm. His tail beat fast against me, almost as rapid as my heart, clearly pleased to see me, but how hadn't he heard me? Because he was locked in the cupboard and his head was covered with the thick hoodie, that's why. He'd been stuffed inside and the door closed, unable to get out.

I lowered him and squatted, stroking his head then checking him over, but he was fine, and very excited. He barked a proper greeting, then glanced at the van and growled, angry at having been imprisoned, but as relieved as me that he was now free and seemingly in fine health. I took out the water and collapsible bowl and poured him a drink which he lapped up rapidly, then took a swig myself and gave him the rest.

"What happened? I was so worried. Are you sure you're okay?"

The little guy barked that he was fine, and to prove it raced around me several times, tongue still dripping water, ears flapping, and all I could do was slump onto my rear and cuddle him as he leapt into my arms.

I wept with relief, unable to stop the surge of emotions. Anxious lapped at my salty tears until I pulled myself together and wiped at my face, smiling down at my best friend in the whole world.

He was safe, we were together again, and he wasn't hurt. I winced as I inadvertently wiped at the lump on my head. One mystery might have been solved, but that still left me with a lot more answers than questions.

Most importantly, where was Ben, and where was the person who had assaulted me then locked Anxious in a cupboard? How had they even done it? I had the key. Ben most likely had another on him and they used that, but why?

"Who was that maniac?" I wondered, but did I really care? This was one mystery I wasn't sure I wanted to get involved in.

Did I have any choice though?

Chapter 3

Stress sloughed from my knotted shoulders like a snake's skin, leaving me feeling like a new man. A butterfly emerged from a chrysalis. I couldn't help but laugh with the intense relief I felt at having Anxious back. My body was light and my mood so jubilant and carefree that I wanted to run around and shout to share my happiness.

I eased my neck from side to side, cricking out the stiffness, then stretched out my back, rolled tense shoulders, and even did a few jumping jacks. I'd always considered myself level-headed and able to keep cool in a crisis, but this had been a worrying wake-up call. With the last of the adrenaline slowly fading, and the knot in my belly easing, I had to accept that when it came to those I loved I was a bag of nerves. At least I'd kept calm enough to think straight once the concussion had lifted, and had found my buddy, but boy had it been a close call.

"What should we do now?" I asked Anxious as he sat staring up at me.

He turned to the van and growled, then yipped a suggestion.

I laughed, then told him, "Arson isn't the answer. There might be clues inside. And it is Ben's home. Not that he said it was."

Anxious barked a question.

"I guess we better go and report it. I haven't got a signal here, so we'd best go to the reception building and explain what happened. We better walk, as my head is still killing me and the last thing we need is for me to drive into a sand dune or run over someone's tent."

As always, the cheery chappy was more than happy to take a walk, so we returned to Vee. I locked up, stuffed water and emergency snacks into my satchel as I hadn't had any lunch yet and despite everything the hunger pangs were beginning to gnaw at me, then we set off back towards the entrance to this incredibly beguiling yet peculiar place.

Munching on a protein bar and sipping water, we made our way towards the group of buildings at the main site. The roads, small tracks, and dead ends were like a maze to my still clearly slightly addled mind, and we took numerous wrong turns, the size of the site still rather mind-boggling after being used to staying at places that were little more than a few fields. Several vehicles passed us, but I didn't try to flag anyone down as I was jittery and way too suspicious to even contemplate getting into a stranger's vehicle.

The day was becoming a true scorcher, surprising for the time of year as May usually brought plenty of great weather, but frost and even snow wasn't unheard of, but this was set to be another heatwave summer and seemingly the sun had decided to go for it early to get some practice in.

Anxious drank a whole bottle of water, and I did likewise, but by the time we finally arrived at the entrance we were both panting. I used a tap to refill the bottles—the sign said it was drinking water—and contemplated going into the shop to buy some cold bottles, and was even more tempted by the on-site pub and restaurant, but left the cheery people sitting at the picnic benches to their meals and pints and headed instead to the reception block.

Thankfully, it was quiet, lunchtime meaning there were no new arrivals at the moment, so I called hello to the woman behind the counter reading a one-pot cookbook—I liked her instantly because of that—and she smiled as she lifted her head.

"Hi. You checked in a few hours ago, right? Is

everything okay? Um, what happened to your head? Are you alright? Take a seat. You look terrible."

"Thanks, I think I better. I'm dizzy." I took the chair indicated and she hurried around the counter of the large room stocked with leaflets advertising local attractions and a fridge full of drinks, the cool interior incredibly welcome. I focused on the tiled floor, for some reason stressing when I noted they didn't all line up how they should, but Anxious barked at me and I snapped back to the present and smiled at him before looking into the eyes of the clearly concerned receptionist.

"Sorry, I was nodding off there. It's so hot outside and it's been a really weird morning."

"Looks like it. That's a hell of a lump you have."

"I got smashed in the forehead by a rifle."

"Very funny," she giggled, brushing a drift of fine jet black hair from her eyes that fell back instantly. Dark eyes sparkled, an arresting focus on her tanned face, catching my attention like they had when we checked in as they were so bright and clear. Lean, bare arms reached out for me and she gripped my shoulders as she studied my head. With a frown, she said, "You might have concussion. Do you feel sick?"

"No, and I think I did, but it's passed now. I had a snack and some water, so I think I'm alright."

"What really happened?"

"I wasn't lying. I was talking to a man in the dunes, then someone in military gear carrying a rifle stormed towards us from out of nowhere, and smashed me in the head. The maniac stole my dog, locked him in a van," Anxious whined to confirm it was true, "and I've no idea where Ben is. I can't figure that guy out. It's been a super weird morning."

The woman frowned, then asked, "Do you mean old Ben? Straggly long hair, wiry type, likes to talk?"

"That's him. He told me he had a brand new van conversion, top of the range, but when I came around and went looking for him, I just found an old Transporter that gave me palpitations. It was so messy. He'd left the key in his tent and I had to go through everything to find it, but I think it's his. Do you know him?"

"Everyone around here knows Ben. Look, not being funny or anything, but are you really alright? You sound utterly mad, you know."

"I know it sounds crazy. Trust me, I'm having a hard time believing it myself. It's all true though. This Ben bloke, what's his story?"

"Ben's what you'd call a local character. Lived locally for years. One of those faces. He was in the army when he was younger, but he's been living here for what must be almost a decade. He was never the same, so they say, not that I knew him before then. He never settled, couldn't keep up with running a home, so someone gave him a van. His old VW Transporter."

"The one I found?"

"I guess. Oh, I'm Tilly. What was your name again?"

"Max. And the little guy, who's desperate for a fuss, is Anxious. And before you ask, it's his name, not his emotional state."

"Um, okay." Tilly shrugged, then squatted and Anxious immediately jumped onto her thighs. She patted his head, but Anxious was having none of that, so flipped over and balanced precariously with his head lolling. "He's a cute little one," laughed Tilly as she rubbed his tummy.

"And he knows it. So, tell me more about Ben."

"I've been working here about five years now, and the owner and other staff told me a little about him. He's what you'd call a compulsive liar. He tells everyone he's got a new van. Been saying the same thing for years. Tells stories about going on missions in the army, but nobody believes him."

"But why lie?"

Tilly shrugged. "It's what he does. Just his way. He's harmless enough. He never has any money, just a few quid now and then, so he mostly stays here. Sure, he comes and goes, but if he's not in his van he's in his tiny tent, or sometimes he takes one of the damaged ones we recycle for people if they want, and fixes it up. Sells it on for a bit of quick cash."

"How does he afford to stay here then? No offence, but it isn't the cheapest in the area."

"No, but it's the best. And he doesn't pay. We let him come and go as he pleases for free. Otherwise, he'd be homeless. He barely scrapes enough together for fuel and keeping that old rust bucket legal, so we look out for him. He gets food from the restaurant most days. We take care of him. He's damaged, Max. If he really was a soldier, then he has PTSD, but even if all that's a lie, something happened to him and he was never the same when he turned up here from wherever he went for almost fifteen years. Mind you, I only know this because of what I've been told."

"And now he's been taken, or worse, by a nutter with a rifle."

"Tell me what happened again? What did they do to Anxious?"

"I got smashed in the head, and when I came around I was alone. I searched the tent, found the key, then the van. His wallet was inside, so I knew it was his. Anxious was locked in a cupboard."

"That's awful! Who would do that?"

"Maybe they knew he'd be found. Anxious would have been barking and going crazy trying to bite the guy, but my guess is all the gear the man wore protected him, so he bundled Anxious inside the van to keep him away while he did whatever he did with Ben."

"Ben's been here for a few days. Before that, he was absent for a couple of weeks. Everyone said it was strange as usually he's never away for so long. We close from October to the end of March to the general public, but he's allowed to stay for those six months, although he usually goes up the coast and pitches at a farm. He helps out there. That's when he earns most of his money. Then he coasts for six months when the weather's better."

"Sounds like a good life."

"Sure, if you can handle being poor, never having enough food, no money to fix your van, and you're getting on in years so physical labour is a struggle. We worry about him. He's a right pain, don't get me wrong, and an absolute nightmare at times, and the constant lying is very trying, but I like him. We all do."

"Think him being abducted has something to do with his army days? Whoever hit me had forces written all over them. The gear was military grade as far as I could tell, and that rifle is a real worry."

"Nobody like that has come through reception, but I'll call the gate house."

"That's where the barrier for entry and exit is, right?"

"Sure. I'll be back in a mo."

I felt woozy so leaned back and rested my head against the wall while Tilly made her call. I must have zoned out as I didn't hear her on the phone, and only came back to the present when she shook my shoulders.

"Sorry, I must have dozed off."

"Max, you didn't doze, you have concussion. You shouldn't sleep, it might be dangerous. You need to be seen by a doctor. You need to go to the hospital."

"I'm fine." I moved to stand, but with a whoosh of blood to the head I slumped back into the chair and admitted, "I think you might be right. Can you call for an ambulance please? And the police. There's an armed man, most likely a kidnapper or worse, on the loose, and who knows what he's doing. Are there other ways on and off the island?"

"Sure. You could hike in if you wanted. The causeway is clear today, no tide to stop you coming and going, but my guess is that the guy came by boat. He could be miles away by now."

"He'd have to carry Ben though. Nobody matching the description I gave left?"

"No, but that doesn't mean much. The guy's hardly

likely to be wearing all his gear and touting a rifle as he asks for the barrier at the exit to be raised, is he? He'd look like any other visitor. If he had Ben in the boot or something, then who would know?"

"True," I admitted, as a wave of sickness threatened to overwhelm me. I felt very tired, and very unwell, and the next thing I knew I blacked out.

It was only for a moment, but as I snapped back to life and stared into the concerned face of the young receptionist, I was admittedly worried.

"Hang in there. I'll call for help right now!"

I nodded, vaguely aware of Tilly standing and jabbing at her phone. Anxious whined from my feet, then scratched at my bare legs, trying to keep me awake.

Wave after wave of tiredness washed over me like the tidal causeway that could stop help arriving, but Tilly had said there were no issues today, hadn't she? I had to stand up, or I knew I'd be comatose, so against everything my mind was insisting was the right course of action, I gripped the chair and heaved up. The dizziness punched me in the head as hard as the rifle had, but I fought it and shook to clear the encroaching fog.

Why did I feel so sick? Was it the heat? Hunger? Yes, I was hungry. I fumbled with my bag and pulled out a pack of emergency biscuits suitable for both man and faithful companion, and tore at the packet, my blood sugar levels crashing. Anxious yipped for joy as the pack split and the contents tumbled to the tiles. I groaned, but managed to stuff the few remaining treats into my mouth, but somehow I'd forgotten how to chew, so was left with a mouthful of dry biscuit I had no idea how to swallow.

Getting my brain into action, I finally managed to eat, the sugar perking me up almost instantly. It was too much, though, and I had to sit, and as I did so I blacked out once more.

When I came to, it was to stare into the eyes of two paramedics. Tilly hovered in the background, glancing at me nervously in-between talking to a police officer. Other people were in the room, too, now, making it claustrophobic and unbearably hot. The paramedics asked me a few questions, told me I definitely had concussion, then I spoke briefly with an officer and explained what had happened before the kind paramedics led me out to a waiting ambulance.

Anxious was going crazy barking in frustration from the ground outside the ambulance, but I was told he wasn't allowed. I stumbled to my feet and explained no way was I going without him, so they permitted him to come but made me swear I would never tell or they'd be in a lot of trouble. The man jumped down, scooped up Anxious who gave him a grateful lick on the nose, then hopped onto the bed with me as the doors were shut and the woman drove us away from Shell Island.

It was a short drive, at least it felt like it, but I wasn't myself and couldn't think straight, so I just clutched Anxious and tried to stay awake.

At the hospital, I thanked the paramedics and got checked in then was put in a room and saw a doctor soon enough. I was told I would have to stay overnight and that the police had questions for me, but they could wait until I'd been checked over properly. They put me on an IV drip and I was given a sandwich and a glass of orange juice then made to sit in a chair and ordered not to fall asleep until I'd had some tests.

It was awful. Not the treatment I received, which was as good as expected from our wonderful NHS staff, but being stuck inside, no view to the outside. The artificial lighting, strange smells, and groans of others on the ward were not things I'd ever enjoyed or was used to. I wanted to see the sea, marvel at the sky, watch people enjoying themselves, but I was trapped in this otherworldly environment and knew I had to do as I was told so I could get better and return to my free, outdoors life.

I panicked, and called for a nurse, asking where Anxious was. She went off to check, then returned with a happy smile and told me that they'd called my next of kin on record and he was with them.

"With Min?" I asked.

"No, it says here that she wasn't available and the other contact was your parents. Jack and Jill. Is that right?"

I stifled a groan and nodded. "Yes, that's correct. They're here?"

"Yes, and by all accounts they're rather a handful."

"Oh, you don't know the half of it. Mum will be demanding a private room and a three-course lunch, I expect. She's probably ordered the doctors to abandon the other patients and make me better instantly or else."

"I'm sure you're exaggerating," she said with a laugh.

"Trust me, if anything I'm downplaying how they are. Any chance we can get rid of them? I'm not really in the mood for my mum. She's, how do I put this delicately, rather loud at times, and quite opinionated."

"I'll see what I can do," said the nurse, winking and smiling.

"Max!"

"Too late," I groaned, as a whirlwind entered the ward, then another dressed in denim followed behind.

"Where's my boy?" demanded Dad.

"Has he had his lunch? He likes pickle, and don't give him anything but sourdough," said Mum to the room at large.

I tried to curl up but they spotted me. "Here we go," I grumbled, and wondered if I could feign a coma until they left.

Chapter 4

"I'll leave you to it," said the nurse with a sympathetic smile, then grabbed her clipboard and studied it intently as she gave my folks a very wide berth.

"Traitor," I hissed, winking even though she couldn't see me.

"My poor boy," said Mum, swishing her black dress, the red polka dots making my eyes hurt. Her hair was a matching crimson, same as her clattering high heels, her make-up flawless as always.

Dad, as much a fifties nut as Mum, hitched up his indigo Levi's 501s, slicked back his greasy dark hair, checked his white tee still had the sleeves rolled up enough to show off his biceps, then shook his head and tutted.

"Hey, guys," I said, trying to look and sound normal or this would not go well.

Dad frowned, and asked, "Max, what happened?"

"Never mind that. Look at him. This boy needs a sandwich, and quick!" Mum spun on her heels, spotted the nurse, and barked, "Hurry, it's a hunger emergency. Cheese and pickle on sourdough, and maybe some crisps. Salt and vinegar. And make sure they're Walker's."

"I don't want crisps," I protested.

"No, but I do. I'm famished." She turned to the startled nurse again and told her, "Make that three sandwiches."

"Lunch was over ages ago. Max has eaten. If you want anything, the cafeteria is open." The nurse marched off, leaving Mum open-mouthed and utterly dumbfounded.

Dad chuckled as he said, "Blimey, that's a first. Did you hear that, Jill? She gave you what for, eh?" Dad winked at me and I stifled a giggle as the temperature plummeted.

"Well I never," hissed Mum, trying to incinerate the nurse with her laser eye, but she ducked out of the ward in time so Mum just burned a hole in the wall opposite.

"Great to see you both," I said, surprising myself by how much I meant it.

"You too, love," cooed Mum, all sympathy. She put her palm to my forehead, whilst reaching behind with her other hand and plumping up the pillow I was trying to relax against. Tutting, she said, "You're too hot. Have you got a fever? Are you ill? They said it was a mild concussion but wouldn't go into detail. We rushed right over as they said poor Anxious was beside himself."

"Is he alright? And I'm fine. I feel okay now. Just a nasty bump to the head."

"It really is," said Dad. "You got clobbered good and proper. Who did it? Another murder mystery?" He rubbed his hands together, clearly keen on the idea.

"Ooh, is it?" screeched Mum. "A murder? Do you know who did it yet?"

"Guys, stop looking so excited about it. And no, there's been no murder. At least, I don't think so."

I explained what had happened, only getting interrupted every few seconds, which was a record for them. When I'd finished, I felt exhausted, and could have happily slept, but knew I wasn't meant to until I'd had a few tests.

"So what happens now?" asked Dad.

"I have to see the doctor, stay the night, then should be fine tomorrow."

"And then we start our investigation," said Mum.

I did a double-take, then put my hands up and said,

"Absolutely not. Leave it to the police. They'll be here soon and I'll have to talk to them, but this isn't your problem." I hoped I could put them off, even though there was no way I could leave this alone, but I knew in my heart I was fighting a losing battle.

"He's gone soft in the head," Mum told Dad. "Totally rattled by that little bump."

"Little bump!?" I blurted, astonished, even though I shouldn't have been, by her change of heart concerning my health.

"You know what I mean." I really didn't. "Son, someone clobbered you and stole a man. And they kidnapped Anxious. We need answers."

"We do, Son. Your Mum's right. And we're here now, so what else can we do? Have to find this liar, Ben, and check he's alright. We'll head back to the campsite, watch over Vee, and have a snoop around."

"I don't think that's a very smart idea."

"No, then what will happen to Anxious? He can't be left alone. He wasn't happy at being told to wait outside while we came to see you, even though we had to stay with him for ages until he settled. He's pining for you."

"I miss him too."

A commotion at the entrance to the ward made us all turn in time to see a very familiar little dog trotting proudly into the room, tail swishing, ears sharp as pins, nose in the air. He spied me and barked, then hurried over with a security guard right on his tail.

"Anxious!" I called, relief flooding my system.

He jumped onto my lap and licked my face manically, tail thumping against Mum's dress.

"How'd he get in here?" asked Dad. "You tied him up, didn't you?" he asked Mum.

"Me? I thought you did it?"

"No, you said that I always did it wrong and to leave it to you."

"I never did."

"Guys, cool it. But do you think it's sensible to be in charge of him if you can't even tie his lead to something? And where is his lead?"

"Are you looking for this?" asked the flustered security guard, the lead dangling from his large hand.

"Yes, sorry about this. I know he shouldn't be in here. Somebody," I shot a glance at my utterly unembarrassed parents, "was meant to keep him outside."

"He needs to leave. It's a health hazard."

"Anxious is not a health hazard," snapped Mum. "He's only tiny, and missed my Max. That's alright, isn't it?"

"Mum, it isn't. It's been great to see you, and thanks so much for coming, but can you please take him outside? It looks like the police are here, anyway, so I better answer their questions."

"We'll go back to the van, Max. Text me the location and we'll check on you later." Dad winked, took Anxious from me, then guided Mum away. She broke free, dashed over, hugged and kissed me, gave the pillow a final adjustment, then snatched the lead from the bewildered security guard and huffed her way to Dad.

"That your Mum? She's a powerhouse isn't she?" said the guard, a wistful look in his eyes. "I like my women strong. She single?"

"Of course she's not single. That was my dad with her." Maybe it was the concussion, as was this guy really smitten, and so oblivious to Dad?

"Shame. Anyway, no more dogs," he warned, then left.

My eyes drifted after him, lazy and unfocused, but sharpened as I watched a man I presumed was a doctor talking with an officer. With a nod, the officer stood back and the doctor approached. He introduced himself, explained that he needed to examine me and do several tests, possibly including a CT scan depending on his findings, but he would start with something called the Glasgow Coma Scale. It sounded worrying until he explained it was to check my memory, balance, how I moved my eyes, and a few other things.

After drawing the curtains around us, he went through everything methodically, noting responses, grunting, re-checking my balance, asking what I was like after the attack, and how I felt, and then explained that I had a mild concussion but the swelling had gone down enough for him be satisfied that I was in no danger and there was no need for anything more but rest. I could go home in the morning after he'd done his rounds and confirmed I was alright. It sounded good to me, although I would have rather left right there and then.

Hospitals are strange places, and always left me on edge when I'd visited people over the years. Now I was the patient it was doubly weird. Here I was, whiling away the hours sitting propped up on the bed now the doctor had said I could rest if I wanted, watching the comings and goings of a busy ward, full of admiration for the staff and the care and attention they gave everyone. The kind words, the assistance, the hope they gave.

What I wasn't as impressed by was dinner. Why would someone responsible for devising a menu for sick people who needed their strength, who had little else to look forward to, think a vegetarian option of mashed potato and cheese and potato bite-sized croquettes was nutritious? Why did the main course for meat-eaters consist of the same potato and unfathomable meat in a sauce and three green beans? Did somebody think it would help restore them to full health? I couldn't figure it out and wondered if I was relapsing, but after talking to the other patients and told that lunch was potato waffles and hash browns, basically double potato again, it became clear that something had gone seriously awry somewhere.

The pressure the NHS was under was understandable, and everyone was working very hard and doing an amazing job, but why was the food still the same as it had been for decades? If anything, it was worse, as we know so much more about the importance of a balanced diet now than we ever did.

I longed for my cast-iron pot and the chance to make a one-pot wonder, and vowed that tomorrow I would make something incredible, taking my time to prepare a meal I was proud of.

Early evening dragged by slowly, but Min called, apologising profusely for not taking the call from the hospital, explaining that she'd been with clients all day, but had heard from Mum and now she was really worried. I put her mind at ease, told her I was fine, and she didn't need to come, even though I would have loved to see her. It might have only been a matter of days since we'd been together, but I missed her terribly even though I didn't say that so she wouldn't worry more.

She asked me a question I hadn't considered yet, which proved I wasn't thinking straight. "Think this is to do with the note you found in your shirt with the name of Shell Island on it?"

"I honestly don't know. I hadn't linked the two."

"Max, that isn't like you. Are you sure the doctor said you were okay?"

"My balance is good now, no neck pain or dizziness. I don't feel sick, can remember everything, and he was happy that I'm fit to leave tomorrow."

"But you didn't consider the attack and note were related?"

"No, and how can they be?"

"You tell me, Max. You tell me. I should come. You need me."

"I will always need you, but I keep telling you, I'm all good. And besides, my folks are here."

"That's exactly why you need me there," she giggled.

I smiled as I pictured her laughing, her cute dimples like two dents in a peach on her rosy cheeks, her lovely blond curls dancing around her angelic face, and I sniffed, thinking of her perfume and shampoo and how familiar and achingly beautiful it was for me.

"Did you just sniff me down the phone? You did,

didn't you? Max, it's weird enough when you do it in person, but over the phone?"

"I did no such thing! You're making it up. Wishful thinking, I reckon," I teased.

"Sleep well, Max, and don't let Jack and Jill stress you out."

"Oh, they will. You can count on it. But don't worry, they mean well and I can handle them."

"Are they staying in Vee?"

"I think so. They were going to guard her. Hopefully, they won't burn her down in the night or do anything dumb."

"They have their own key, don't they?"

"Yes, in case of emergencies, as they put it. Let's hope they look after her."

"I'm sure they will. I'll see you soon. Love you."

Min hung up before I had the chance to tell her I loved her too.

I spent the next few minutes lost in a dream of a possible future with Min, knowing we were approaching our deadline in a few months. No, it was weeks away now, wasn't it? As I tried to crunch the numbers, the officer from earlier coughed politely and apologised for the delay, but said he'd been called away. He wanted to ask me a few questions, so I agreed, and spent the next hour going over everything in detail, then repeating things for a second time so he could be sure my memory was working properly and I missed nothing out.

By the end of it, I was exhausted, and couldn't wait for him to leave.

"What happens now?"

"Teams are already investigating. There is no sign of Ben, but his van has been found and we used the key you left at the campsite to gain access. It's all as you say. There is no sign of him or the person who assaulted you and stole your dog, although we can't be a hundred percent certain he took the animal or Ben. The entire island has been checked, but there is no sign of anything untoward. A missing persons case has been opened, but so far there is nothing to go on."

"Thanks for letting me know. What should I do tomorrow? Is a detective involved? Anyone I know?"

"Why would you know them, sir?"

After explaining about my history, and having dealings with a mystery in Harlech, the officer checked up on me then grinned. "Ah, that Max. I've heard talk of you, but not to worry as so far this is more of an informal inquiry if you get my drift."

"Not really, no. Isn't there a lead detective? There was someone with a weapon."

"Yes, and it's being looked into. No offence, Max, but we only have your word for it. Ben is a known local character and I've dealt with him a few times myself. Nothing bad, just when he's been parked where he shouldn't be. He often disappears for days at a time, a real loner type, and sometimes gets into a bit of bother. Usually not having money to pay for petrol or some shopping and we get called out, but rest assured everything that can be done is being done."

I must have drifted off then as when I woke up the officer was gone and the ward was quiet.

I listened to the hum of machines, the regular beeps of things I assumed were meant to go beep, and the endless rounds of the nurses checking on patients at regular intervals. The place never seemed to stop entirely, and lights always shone. How were people meant to get a proper night's sleep with so much activity?

Nevertheless, I drifted off eventually, and was surprised to find it was seven AM when I woke up. In desperate need of the bathroom, I realised I hadn't gone since the afternoon before, which couldn't be good. Maybe it was because the pressure was off. Living in a van meant I always had to go right before bed, then the minute I snuggled down I started thinking about if I'd need to go in the night, so ended up having to get straight back up and pee again. Then I'd wake at least once, if not twice in the night and have to go again.

Toilet facilities, or the lack of them, were the main drawback to living in a small van without any spare room, but I had come to a compromise of late and now used a specially designed bottle that solved having to get out of Vee. I knew plenty of other vanlifers or campers struggled with the same issue, women more so, so now there were a whole plethora of portable toilets and specially designed bottles and funnels and other things most people didn't want to talk about that could help solve the issue.

That didn't mean I didn't hurry with all due haste to the bathroom!

Back at my bed, I sorted through my bag, not much there to sort, then sat in the chair and waited for the doctor to arrive. He didn't do his rounds until nine, so I had breakfast of cereal and toast, then zoned out. After he checked me over, he gave me the all clear, and signed me off as fit to leave, so I thanked him and the nurses then left.

Or tried to.

As much as I was certain I was following the signs, I still got lost twice and had to ask directions. Frustrated, and aching for daylight, I whooped as I stepped out of the shade of the entrance and thanked my lucky stars that my stay had been short, unlike so many who were receiving treatment for serious illnesses and might be bedridden for weeks or months.

What to do now? Call my folks for a lift, or get a taxi? Where was I anyway? After checking on the hospital sign, wondering how I hadn't thought to ask, then realising I was most likely told yesterday when I was rather unwell, I decided a walk into town would do me good. I could grab a coffee before deciding what to do.

The walk was exactly what I needed, and cleared my head. After sitting outside a cafe and enjoying the coffee and the sunshine, I called Min to let her know I was fine, then called my folks and told them I'd get a taxi. They were having a great time, apparently, and had walked along the beach with Anxious last night and this morning, but the little guy was missing me and wouldn't let them have any room in the bed, so they hadn't slept well. I hung up and chuckled at the thought of Anxious spread-eagled on the pillows, hogging all the space while Mum and Dad tried to cope with the already cramped sleeping arrangements.

    Time to go home.

Chapter 5

"Anxious!" I crouched and the little guy yipped for joy then tore from the gazebo and raced across the scrub. He leaped onto my lap where I squatted, licking manically, tail thudding against my legs as he whined and wiggled, his innocent joy and the fearless way he expressed his emotions making my heart soar.

"He missed you," said Dad as he wandered over, dragging his steel comb through his already perfect hair then tucking it in his back pocket.

"And I missed him. Have you been a good boy for Grandad?"

"Grandad? That makes me sound old."

"Sorry, but you know what I mean."

"I do, Son, and it's alright. I can be Grandad. Just don't call your mother Grandma or we'll have a problem."

"I know better than that," I said with a smile and a wink. Dad and I both knew what the real meaning of this conversation was. He would never be a true grandfather and it saddened him and Mum, but they felt much more sad for me and Min.

"Great to see you, Dad." I let Anxious down, then stood and hugged the man who had done so much for me in my life and had always been there for me no matter what.

"You too, Son. I told you we'd come and get you. We have our car so we wouldn't have to drive Vee."

"It's fine." We broke and stood back from each other because Anxious wasn't finished being excited and kept pushing between our legs, so I calmed him until he was satisfied then he wandered back to the pitch to check on Grandma, I mean Mum!

"What did the doctor say? Are you all good? The lump's gone down."

"He said I was fine yesterday, but just kept me in overnight to be sure. I feel great today. Back to normal. Thanks for coming. I appreciate it."

"For you, anything, you know that. It's been a nice change, and we had fun with Anxious. That dog never gets tired, though, does he? He walked for hours yesterday and this morning." Dad checked there were no eavesdroppers, then moved close and whispered, "Your mum even took her shoes off on the beach after a few miles. We had a paddle, and she said the sand felt lovely on her bare feet."

"No way! Mum never takes her shoes off. Sometimes I wonder if she goes to bed in them."

"Occasionally she does. But only on special Thursdays when we both—"

"I do not want to hear about that!" I gasped, shaking my head to clear the visions before they took hold.

"Suit yourself." Dad shrugged. "But we're only in our fifties, Max, and have a very active s—"

"No, again, don't want to hear about it. Did you sleep alright?" I smirked as he sighed, panic in his eyes.

"We did not! It was awful. Anxious was whining half the night and kept sniffing the pillows. He took up nearly all the room. Your mum snored even though she'll insist she didn't get a wink of sleep, and having to go outside for a pee is a nightmare. How do you cope?"

"I have a pee bottle."

"Fair enough, but it isn't ideal, is it? What are you going to do when Min moves in?"

"If she moves in."

"Don't be daft, Son. Course she will. We love Min

and can't wait for you two to be a proper family again. Will you manage in the little van?"

"She's stayed plenty of times, remember? We do just fine. It's cramped, but the freedom makes up for it and we both love Vee. Anxious does too."

"We all do. She's a great van, but whatever way you look at it it's tiny. I know I've asked you before, but would you settle in a house if Min wanted to?"

"And my answer is the same. Of course I would. I'd do anything for her, you know that. I love this life, but I love her more. It would be different this time around anyway. I think if we had a house we'd hardly ever be inside. We both adore being out in all weathers and wherever we end up, the great outdoors would be the focus."

"You should run a campsite. That would be perfect for you both. That way, you could both camp or sleep in Vee as much as you wanted. Or at least a property with land, so there's space for the van."

"That's a great idea, Dad, and I'd love to run a campsite. We'd live in Vee and get to meet lots of new people, earn money, and look after a piece of land. Let's just see what the future holds, eh?"

"Sure thing, Son. I'm just relieved you're well. Come on, your mother will be out soon." Dad put his arm around my shoulder, although it was rather awkward for him as I didn't inherit my height from either of my folks.

We wandered back over to the pitch as I asked, "Is Mum refreshing her make-up?"

"Yeah, and changing after our walk, and seeing how much mess she can make in your van."

"She's awful. How can she ever find anything? She's so messy."

"It's just her way, Son. A happy marriage is about compromise. Your mother looks after me, runs the home, cooks, cleans, all of that, so I pick up after her, put things away, do the garden and the DIY and tell her I love her every single morning when we wake up and every single night when I kiss her goodnight. We're a team."

"You are, and I'm proud of you both. You taught me so much about how to live a happy life, yet I still ignored it and went off the rails."

"You're young, just in your thirties, and got carried away with dreams of money and recognition doing something you love. I get it. I knew you'd see sense eventually. Maybe a little late, as you pushed it so far Min ditched you, but you're back on track now and we're both very proud of you. Min too."

"Thanks, Dad. That means a lot. I'm sorry I let you down. I never meant to. I lost my way and didn't even realise until it was too late, but things are different now."

"They sure are, and what a change to your life it's been, eh? Ours too. It broke our hearts seeing you so sad and stressed all the time, and after the divorce we worried about your mental health. Well done for pulling yourself back from the brink and starting again. It's a real achievement and we couldn't be happier."

"You've always been so supportive. I don't know what I'd have done without you over the years."

"Messed up even bigger." Dad laughed, then slapped me on the back, and we both took a step back as a vision in a polka dot dress squeezed through the van door, stepped down using the little fold-up step, and frowned at us.

"Well?" asked Mum with a wicked scowl that sent Anxious crawling on his belly under Vee and us unable to move as we were caught in the glare.

"Well what?" asked Dad bravely.

"Hi, Mum. Lovely to see you. You look pretty. Is that a new dress? It's very, er, yellow, with lovely red polka dots. Matches your yellow shoes. New too?"

"Of course they're new, and neither of you said anything after the trouble I've gone to. Does it clash with my red hair?"

"Only in a very endearing way, love," said Dad, stepping behind me.

"And we did say how incredible you looked. The moment you appeared I said it."

"I was there for ages." Mum pouted, but couldn't keep it up for long, and a smile spread across her line-free face and she swished her way over then hugged me tight, her head resting on my chest. "My boy's home and safe. That's all that matters. Plus, you said I looked nice. Not like him."

Dad squeaked like a mouse, then peered around me and said, "You look as divine as always, my love. Beautiful. Let the boy go or you'll suffocate him."

Mum released me, stood back, and frowned at Dad as she asked, voice ominously low, "Are you saying I'm fat? That I could squeeze our son who is six one and who knows how many pounds until he dies? That I would murder my own child because I'm obese?"

"What!? Course not! You're the perfect size. Lovely and curvy in all the right places."

I tutted at Dad as I shook my head, but he'd already realised the massive error he'd made and stepped away as Mum's head swivelled a full three-sixty and the lasers fired up. "So you do think I'm fat?"

"No, like I said. Perfect. Shall I make coffee?" Dad asked hurriedly, then sidestepped to the kitchen and began filling the kettle.

Mum winked at me and whispered, "Gotta keep him on his toes," then dragged me out into the sunshine away from Dad so we could talk in private while he pretended not to notice.

"I'm so glad you're safe and recovered."

"Thanks, Mum. It was a shock, for sure, and I was so worried about Anxious. But I'm absolutely fine, so don't worry."

"You know I'll always worry. It doesn't matter how old you get, you'll always be my little boy."

"I know." I kissed her forehead and hugged her.

"Now, let's get down to business."

"What business?"

"Of finding who did this to you. We're going to, right?"

"I don't think that's a good idea. He had a rifle. He attacked me and kidnapped Anxious. Who knows what happened to Ben, but the police didn't find anything. He's vanished."

"We saw the police yesterday. There were loads of them going all over the island. We spoke to lots of people and the police were very active talking to visitors and checking vans and cars and they even had officers at the harbour. Anxious was sad, though, as he saw the children crabbing and wanted a go, but we didn't have the right equipment."

"Then let's go crabbing later. Maybe after lunch. You didn't pester the police or other campers, did you?"

"Me?" Mum managed to look affronted even though we both knew there was no way she and Dad hadn't been bending the ears of everyone they could find, including the police.

"Yes, you," I laughed.

"We might have had a quick chat with a few people. Just a word, nothing more."

"A likely story! So, what did you find out?"

"That this Ben character is a big, fat liar. He tells everyone he has a swanky new van but only has that old rust bucket. He was in the army apparently, away for a long time, but came back ages ago and was never quite the same. Everyone seems to like him and he gets to stay here for free and works up at a local farm. He stays there when the campsite is closed sometimes, but they let him stay here if he wants."

"That's what I was told yesterday by the woman at reception."

"Ah, Tilly," beamed Mum. "A lovely girl. She was very helpful. Told us about you going there yesterday. She called for help."

"She was great. You didn't go to Ben's van, did you?"

"Of course we did! Why wouldn't we? We had to try to find out what happened. It's still there, you know. The police didn't take it. The nice officers who were going through everything told us they wouldn't take it away in case Ben returned. It has his stuff in it. They said maybe he just wandered off after the attack."

"Why would anyone come to attack him though? There's something very weird going on, obviously, but nobody seems to know what."

"Exactly! That's why you need our help. Ooh, I do love a murder mystery."

"It's not a murder. There's no body."

"Maybe, or maybe not," said Mum cryptically. "Maybe there is and we haven't found it yet." She grinned, and rubbed her hands together, then smoothed down her immaculate dress and checked her matching yellow bandanna was perfect before taking my arm. "Lets have a coffee, then we can make lunch, and you boys can do your crabbing. It'll be fun."

"Okay," I said warily, knowing she was up to something, also knowing there was absolutely nothing I could do about it. Once Mum made up her mind about something, she would not be swayed from her path. Ever.

With the stress of the previous day and the peculiar after-effects of my brief stint in hospital fading, until I could release the thoughts and focus on the present, we had a nice hour enjoying each other's company, drinking coffee, eating a simple lunch, and catching up on gossip.

Mum and Dad loved to keep me up-to-date on the local news, going into way too much detail about the neighbours, the places they'd been, the dances they attended. They'd gone ballroom dancing for decades, strictly fifties style, and attended numerous other events based around their favourite era, and I heard about them all while we sat in the sun. Anxious tried to stay awake for treats, but was clearly exhausted by the upset and soon retreated to his favourite spot under Vee where it was nice and cool and he could play den.

After lunch, and without my folks protesting as they knew me well enough to not bother arguing, I set about cleaning up the horrendous state of the kitchen then braved it and cautiously approached Vee. One glimpse through the open door and I knew I had my work cut out for me.

"Don't worry, Son, we've got other sleeping arrangements for tonight, so your mother won't make a mess again."

"I do not make a mess. It's because there's no room."

I turned from Vee and asked Mum, "How is it possible for one tiny woman to cause such carnage in a single night? How do you manage to get more make-up than Boots stock into a tiny van? And what do you need it all for?"

Mum grinned and waved a hand over her face, indicating her make-up, as if that was enough of an answer. "Ta-da!"

I shook my head in wonder at this whirlwind of a woman, then asked, "What arrangements? You're welcome to stay here, you know that. I'll sleep in the gazebo. I don't mind."

"No, we know you like your quiet time, so we'll leave after you've cooked us an awesome one-pot wonder."

"Deal," I agreed, hoping I didn't answer too hastily.

"Max," called Dad, "just bring our stuff out. We'll load the car so it's ready to go later."

"But I might need my make-up," protested Mum.

"Then you can do it in the car. Max needs his home back. We should have been more considerate. He's just out of hospital and now he has to tidy up."

"Be careful of my dresses," warned Mum.

"How many did you bring?" I asked, daring not to look again.

For once, Mum was silent. Never a good sign.

The lovely original sixties retro interior of my beloved 67 VW Campervan was hidden beneath a veritable mountain of dresses. Some were strewn on the rock n roll bed, others hung from hangers, more were draped over the seats, and every available inch of surface was covered in make-up, brushes, bandannas, even shoes. How Mum hadn't become a true hoarder living in a house rammed floor-to-ceiling with stuff was testament to Dad's unending patience and his love for her.

I set to work, and thankfully Dad waited just outside Vee to take things off me as I passed them out, while Mum hummed merrily to herself, occasionally "helping" by stating that she didn't see what the fuss was about and it was only a few dresses.

I didn't even ask how long it had taken them to pack up before they came to visit, and how long it took to load everything into Vee, but by the resigned look on Dad's face, it was clearly much longer than he'd have liked.

Still, half an hour later it was done and I was wiping down the last of the surfaces and removing a stubborn streak of bright red lipstick that had clearly decided to go for a walk.

Next came the much more trying ordeal of waiting while Mum "freshened up" in her own inimitable style. It didn't matter that she'd only got ready a short while ago, a trip anywhere meant everything had to be gone over for any sign of imperfections. Dad and I were old hands at this, so sorted what we needed then had a cuppa and a chat while we waited.

Finally, it was time to go, so I grabbed the crabbing gear, we locked the vehicles, reminded Anxious to stay close and not pester anyone for food, and headed off to the estuary where boats were moored and the handy map indicated was the best crabbing spot.

It was quite a walk, but it was lovely to stretch my legs, feel the sun on my skin, and smile and nod at others out to enjoy this fine day. Everyone was in good spirits, strolling, riding bikes, walking dogs, encouraging kids to hurry to the water, and the time passed quickly until we finally arrived at the estuary where the land was often cut off, giving Shell Island it's name. Today the water was low, and boats sat hunkered down in the silty shallows, listing to one side, the smell of fish and salt and freedom and life so familiar yet always so full of promise I smiled and felt my worries vanish.

Chapter 6

The harbour was busy, but not unduly so. The size of the island meant there was more than enough room for everyone, so we stood and watched the boats for a while, until Anxious whined and I agreed we could do some crabbing.

I'd always been in two minds about this strange and somewhat esoteric art. Catching a fish with a hook then either releasing it or killing it to eat never sat quite right with me, although I'd certainly done my fair share and sometimes even enjoyed the peace it afforded. Crabbing was a compromise, but still a peculiar thing to do.

Kids revelled in the act, though, and were squealing with delight as they hauled in their nets with a weighted small string bag attached where you put a piece of bacon to entice the crabs. I went and filled the little bucket with water so we could put the crabs we caught in it, then returned to the eager faces of Mum, Dad, and Anxious.

Dad had sorted out the bacon and had unwound the line, so Anxious took the nylon in his mouth, walked to the edge with the net, then carefully lowered it over the rocks we stood on and into the water. He kept lowering until the line went slack, then let go and Dad reeled in the rest and held on so everything didn't get tangled.

Anxious barked a question.

"No, you have to wait longer than that!" I laughed. "Give it a few minutes. You have to let the crabs find the bacon, then try to get a nibble."

Anxious nodded, then wandered off, already bored.

"He needs to learn some patience. What do you think, love?" asked Dad, eyes on the line. We turned when Mum didn't answer, to find her walking away in the opposite direction, muttering to herself about boys and their silly toys.

"Guess someone else does too," I chuckled.

"Wonder if we'll catch any?"

"I bet we will. Make sure to let Anxious pull the net in though."

"Of course. It's the little guy's catch, not mine."

Dad was clearly having fun, so I took in my surroundings, admiring the boats and the view across the estuary, considering a day trip to neighbouring Harlech or possibly Barmouth. Both had great beaches, but Barmouth had a funfair and arcade, plus more shops, and I was keen to buy an oggie, a type of Welsh pasty that they sold in a tiny shack close to the railway station and always went down a treat.

As I stood there, listening to the gulls screech and Dad gasp every time he saw a bubble in the water, wondering out loud if a crab had taken the bait, something began to gnaw at me. Not a crab, but an insistent nagging of a yet-to-form thought. I knew the feeling, and didn't force it, rather just let it slowly coalesce until there it was.

Could it be true? Had the police overlooked this? Had I? I tried to think back to what I'd seen, but realised I couldn't as I'd been delirious and concussed, stressed beyond belief about Anxious, and not paying as much attention as I usually would. With a very keen eye for detail, the image was there now, though, and I was beginning to put a few pieces of a puzzle that would be nowhere near solved together.

It could wait a while, though, as I didn't want to spoil the fun. Anxious had endured enough, so deserved this. I returned to Dad and Anxious and Mum came over, too, keen to see what we'd caught.

"Care to do the honours?" Dad asked Anxious.

He wagged, and approached carefully, mindful of the line, then grabbed it between his teeth and carefully pulled back until he'd hauled the net from the water and onto the rocks.

With a bark, he let go and we crowded around to see three small crabs feeding off the bacon.

"Well done, Anxious," beamed Dad, winking at me.

"Great job, buddy," I said, patting his head.

Anxious sat, head cocked, and looked at me.

"It's up to you, but you know what happened last time."

Anxious stood, edged forward cautiously, then bared his teeth, prepared to gently grab a crab and put it in the bucket of sea water. The moment he got close enough, a crab reached out with a pincer and locked onto his twitching nose. Anxious yowled in pain, although it was such a small crab it couldn't have been that bad, and raced around, shaking his head as he tried to dislodge it.

Despite our laughter, and the fact he'd done the same thing last time, I chased after the little guy and scooped him up then carefully prised the bewildered crustacean free and dropped it into the water before doing the same with the others.

Anxious whined and batted at his nose, but he'd live, and maybe this time he'd learned his lesson.

"Did you have fun?" I asked, stifling a laugh.

Anxious wagged happily and barked that he had, then trotted over to the bucket and began to stick his nose in the water.

"Whoa there, crazy fella," Dad warned, and pulled him away. "Didn't you learn anything?"

"I think he enjoyed the attention," said Mum. "Can we go now please? I fancy having a nice sit down this afternoon and maybe a quick snooze. It's such a lovely day. Then we can begin our investigation properly later on."

"Of course we can go. But how are you going to

begin the investigation?" I asked, despite knowing better.

"Never you mind," Mum huffed, clearly having no idea where to start.

"We need to make a slight detour on the way back," I told everyone. "Something's come up and it might be important."

"Max knows something!" declared Dad, clapping his hands. "What is it, Son? A clue? Do you know who did it?"

"It might be a clue, or it might be more than that. Let's wait and see."

Anxious picked up the bucket by the handle and followed me to the water, then tipped it over so the crabs could return to safety for a while until they fell for the same bacon trick again. I sorted everything out, threw the bacon in as they deserved it, then we retraced our steps for quite a while before veering off into the dunes.

"Where are we going, Son?" asked Dad.

"Is it far? My feet are tired."

"Not far. Bear with me, okay?"

They nodded, having full faith in me as always, and a few minutes later we arrived at Ben's van.

"This old rust bucket again," moaned Mum. "It hurts my eyes to look at it. Why are we here?"

"Just stay where you are for a moment and let me explain, then follow me. You came here yesterday, right?"

"Just to have a look at where poor Anxious was kidnapped and to see if we could find any clues. He didn't like it." Dad turned to Anxious, who was lying down, paws over his eyes.

"It's okay, you don't have to look," I told him. "Sorry about this, but I think it's important. I'll need your help in a moment." Anxious lifted his head and grunted, then covered his eyes again.

"Look over there," I told my folks. "I know the footprints are messed up now, but yesterday I traced the steps of the person I'd seen until we lost them. Now there are loads more after the police came to check things out, but look at the tire marks. You can still just make them out. The van was shunted back and forth, going over the same ground. It was driven forward then back a few times. It left a deep impression."

"So this Ben guy wanted to get the perfect spot." Dad shrugged.

"You wouldn't go back and forth like that if you wanted to change where you parked. I think it's for another reason."

"Me. Me!" wailed Mum, putting her hand up like I was a teacher and would pick her.

"Yes, you over there in the lovely dress," I said, winking at Dad who stifled a smirk.

"Was it because the killer did it?"

"Exactly! Well done. Extra dinner for you tonight."

"Yes!" Mum pulled a face at Dad, then danced a cringe-inducing jig to tease him.

"I was going to say that too. But, um, why did he move the van? And how? You found the key in the tent."

"Maybe Ben had two sets. Most people do. He must have, as the van was locked when I found Anxious inside. And the van was moved because someone wanted to put something underneath it," I said. "He clearly wanted the van parked directly over it so had to go back and forth a few times until he was satisfied. We need to check."

"But we don't have a key for the van," said Mum. "You gave it to the police."

"I know, but Dad can break in and hot-wire it, right?"

"Easy. You know what we're like with losing things, so I can do it no problem. Not with modern vehicles, but I could do this with my eyes closed. Maybe the killer did the same."

"You are brilliant at getting us out of a pickle," said Mum. "I don't know where our keys keep going to, but Jack's great at sorting things out."

Dad used his comb, a piece of wire on his wallet

chain, and was inside in a flash. A few seconds later, he'd started the van and driven it forward then turned off the engine.

He unlocked the back door for me and I retrieved the small foldable army shovel I'd spied the day before, so I assembled it then stood on the spot where the van had been.

"Ready?" I asked.

"Son, if there's something here, shouldn't we call the cops?"

"They won't come just because I say I think that maybe there's a clue here. Why would they?"

"Because you're usually right?" suggested Mum.

"They don't know that, silly," said Dad.

"I am not silly!"

"We need to give them a reason to come, and I think I know what that is. Mum, you might want to look away. Anxious, can you help please?"

"Why would I want to look away?" Contrarian that she was, Mum marched over and loomed despite her stature. Her presence more than made up for her height.

"Love, I think what Max is trying to say is that it might be gross. You know, body parts, or worse."

"What could be worse than body parts?" asked Mum.

"Inside parts?" suggested Dad, shivering despite the heat.

"Guys, I don't know what we'll find, if anything, but I wanted to give you a heads-up. Mum, are you sure? It might give you nightmares."

"I can handle a bit of grossness. The only thing that gives me nightmares is seeing your Dad's old Y-fronts."

"I do not have old Y-fronts. I might have a few pairs of classics, but they aren't nasty or anything."

"Suit yourselves."

Anxious waited patiently for them to stop bickering, then stepped forward bravely, despite the proximity of the van. He glanced at it and growled, hackles raised, then turned back to me.

I began to dig, and he did likewise, using his paws to rapidly scoop out the loose sand and soil combo. The shovel was sharp and in good condition, but well worn, and it made short work of the ground. I took it slowly and carefully, not wanting to make a mess of anything, but knew it had to be done.

Within minutes, I came into contact with something and asked Anxious to stop. Mum and Dad joined me on my hands and knees and carefully we began to smooth away the ground around what was obviously Ben. It didn't take long to uncover from his shirt up to his head. I brushed the last of the dirt from his face and Mum gasped and Dad gripped my arm tightly as I sank back onto my haunches and sighed.

"He definitely got murdered then," noted Dad.

"There's no doubt about it," I agreed.

"Especially with a hole right in the middle of his forehead," said Mum. "Think you could get your finger in it?"

Dad and I turned to her in shock and stared.

"What? I wasn't going to do it." Mum glanced at her poised index finger, the red nail shining, then lowered it with a grin. "I had an itch."

"Why would you even ask that question?" Dad shook his head and tutted.

"Mum, that's super weird even for you."

"I just wondered. It's quite big, but perfectly in the middle of the poor man's head. Would the bullet have gone right through?"

Dad and I shrugged.

"I have no idea," I said, "but I suppose it would have. I don't know enough about rifles or their power, or the difference bullets make. But either way, Ben's dead."

"Well done." Dad slapped me hard on the back.

"For what? I didn't save him."

"No, but you found him. Now we can get justice. At least people won't give up on him and put it down as just one of those things. Of course, it would be better if he was fine, but that was very unlikely after what happened."

"True. This is so weird. Why on earth would someone come after him and kill him like this? Why do it at the campsite when he could wait until Ben was somewhere quieter? Or at least do it at night. He knocked me out, kidnapped Anxious, moved the van around, and had to get away. It's a real puzzler."

"The killer knew Ben would most likely stay here for a while but wanted him gone. Maybe he came to take something off Ben and it was so important he had to kill him. Maybe something to do with the army? We should find out more about Ben's past and what he was really up to. He worked up at a farm, you said. That's a good place to start."

"I agree with all of that. But should we? I'll worry about you two. Maybe you should go home so I know you're safe."

"Max, we aren't going anywhere," said Mum. "You say you'll worry about us if we stay, but how do you think we'd feel if we left? We wouldn't sleep a wink. We're staying, and we're going to help."

"If you're sure?"

"We are," said Dad, kissing Mum and squeezing her hand.

"What was that for?" she asked him.

"For being such a great mum and a wonderful wife."

As before, I had no signal, so we returned to Vee then I drove up to the entrance and entered the reception building. Tilly was seeing to a customer so I waited until they'd left.

"Me again," I said with a smile. "Thanks for everything you did yesterday. I appreciate it. And I understand you met my folks?"

"Yes, they're, er, chatty, aren't they?"

I laughed, and agreed, "Yes, very."

"Are you okay now? I was worried about you."

"I'm fine, thanks. Look, there's been a development. I found Ben. I got a feeling something wasn't right about his van, that possibly it had been moved. We, um, hot-wired it and shifted it and dug under and found him. He's been shot in the head."

Tilly turned green, and held on to the counter for support, then asked, "You're sure?"

"Absolutely. I assume by whoever whacked me yesterday. Can you call the police again?"

"Yes, of course. The signal's been so iffy lately, but usually we have great reception."

"It's probably the heat playing havoc with the masts. I'm sorry about this. I know you thought a lot of Ben. Before you call, can I ask you a few questions?"

"Sure, I guess. Like what? Poor Ben, I really did like him. He's always been around ever since I started here. Always good for a chat, even if it usually became outlandish."

"That's what I wanted to ask. Did you know anyone from his past? Where he used to live? Parents? Family or friends who know what he was like before, or any army buddies? This is screaming that the guy who did it was ex-forces, so it would be good to have a starting point."

"You're going to try and solve it, aren't you? I looked you up, Max, or rather, your dad showed me the wiki page he'd made for you. That's very impressive. I know you said you'd been involved in a few things around here, but wow. You're either very unlucky, or very lucky, depending on how you view these things."

"I'm still struggling with knowing the answer to that question. Both, I suppose."

"As for Ben, I know he worked at the farm part of the year, but nobody knows anything about his past. Even people who have been here their whole lives don't know. It seems the most likely explanation is that he moved here in his early twenties, mooched about for a bit, mostly camping, then went off and joined the army before returning. I'm not sure this is his hometown. He could have been raised anywhere."

"Friends?"

"None that anyone knows of. I asked around last night and today. He knew lots of people, but was a loner. Liked his own company. Nobody really understood him or why he lied so much about everything. It put people off, you know?"

"Sure, I get it."

"You never knew where you stood with him. He'd tell a blatant lie but never admit it. It got annoying. He was a genuinely nice guy though. Please figure out who did it."

"I'll try my best."

Tilly made the call while I stepped outside as suddenly the room felt ice cold.

Chapter 7

Tilly hung up with a frown as she came outside.

"Everything okay?"

"I guess. That was weird. I called 999 and was told to hold, then I was put through to the local station and told to wait again."

"That is weird."

"I haven't got to the odd part yet. I spoke to a detective, and he was really nice, but he told me that officers would arrive soon to secure the scene. He insisted that nobody was to touch anything, but also that you weren't to leave here until you'd given a statement to an officer. Then you were to go for a very long walk on the beach with whatever crazies were with you and that the detective refused to see or speak to you. They're still smarting from the incident at the vets over in Harlech, no doubt, not that the guy said that. Just that you were to remain by reception, give a statement, explain everything, then, and these are his words, bugger off with that smart little dog of his and stay out of our way. Sound about right?"

"Yeah, unfortunately it does. I guess I'll wait here then."

"We could always get a drink. The pub's right here so we may as well. I bet you need one, don't you?"

"I wouldn't mind something cold and alcoholic," I admitted.

Tilly made a few calls and I phoned Dad to tell him I'd be a while, then after Tilly's cover arrived we wandered over. It was a nice place, bustling with people, so we headed to the bar and Tilly introduced me to the barman, a friendly guy in his forties named Tim who took our orders, refused any money, then served the next customer.

We took a seat at a just-vacated picnic bench outside, the sun cheery on this now rather ominous day.

"What did the owner say?" I asked Tilly. "Did you call them?"

"Of course. They said to go along with whatever the police wanted, but they'd already spoken to them yesterday and given any information they requested. They said if we need to shut down, then do it, but don't think it will come to that."

"It wouldn't be easy to close this place, would it?"

"Nigh on impossible. There are people everywhere, thousands of them, all walking, swimming, paddle boarding, or out for day trips in the area. You'd never do it. Max, that was weird about the detectives, wasn't it? What did you do to them?"

"Nothing. It was a rather intense incident at the vets and I ended up figuring out who committed the crime before they did, and I guess if they've been following along with my wiki page since then they know I've been involved in a few more unusual incidents. Maybe they don't want to risk me beating them to it again."

"And you're going to try?"

"I don't know what else I can do now. I admit that it has me intrigued, and no way do I want this killer to get away with it. It's not just that though."

"It's personal now, right? They took your dog."

"Exactly. I would never sleep again if this guy wasn't found. Not only are they a cold-blooded killer, but they're the kind of person who would lock a defenceless animal in a van cupboard on a swelteringly hot day. Anxious could have died."

"Then I hope you find out who did it. I'd take their advice, though, and steer clear until they've done their searches and removed poor Ben's body. No point rubbing them up the wrong way."

"I will. Can I rely on you to fill me in on all the details though?"

"Of course. I'll do whatever I can to help. I have your back."

"Great." I sipped my cool cider, the perfect antidote to the stress I suddenly felt under.

"Hey, there's Russell. He might be able to help us out." Tilly shouted out to a man clutching a pint of something dark. He turned and smiled as he waved, then changed direction and headed towards us.

"Who is he?"

"Probably the closest thing to a friend Ben ever had. At least that I know of. He's quite flaky like Ben, but a kind man. Another one who stays for free and is a regular face around the area."

I studied him as he walked over. A slight limp made his gait a little off, but it would be easy to overlook. He wore very faded knee length cut-offs, with a green vest. He was barefoot. One of the most tanned people I had ever seen, he clearly had more melanin than most Brits and spent most of his time outside. With leather bracelets, rings on his fingers, faded tattoos all over his arms and hands, and long hair streaked with grey, I put him at about Ben's age, mid-to-late-fifties, but the deeply etched lines on his friendly face could have been from sun damage more than age or a hard life.

"Hey. What's up?" Russell smiled quizzically at Tilly, then turned and nodded to me. "Hi."

"Hi. I'm Max, a new friend of Tilly's."

"Nice to meet you. I know who you are though. Tilly, this is the guy, right?"

"It is. Russell, will you take a seat and have a chat?"

"Sure. Be glad to." Russell eased onto the bench

beside Tilly, wincing as he lifted his left leg, but smiling the whole time. "Terrible news about Ben going missing yesterday. And I'm so sorry about your dog. It sounded awful. How's the head?"

"Much better now, thanks."

"Russell, we have some bad news."

He lifted his pint and drained a third before sighing and saying. "I was expecting as much. You don't get attacked by a gunman in the dunes and it end happily. Is he dead?"

"He is. Max here found him not long ago. He's buried in the sand by his van. Nobody else thought to look underneath it, but Max did."

"That's smart. Damn, I liked that guy. Sure, he was a handful and an incorrigible liar, but we were good buddies. How did he die?"

"He was shot in the head. Right here." I pressed my finger to my forehead and winced as it was close to my bruise.

Russell shook his head and rubbed at his forehead, as though he, too, could feel the impact of the bullet. "Terrible business. Me and him were alike. Loners. Never had any money, no proper home, no family of our own, or real friends."

"Hey, you have us here. We're your friends." Tilly squeezed his hand and he smiled warmly at her.

"Thank you. You know what I mean though. Some of us can't seem to get on in the modern world. It's too confusing. I like a simple life and they've always been good to me here," he told me. "I mostly sleep in my tent, sometimes the car, and it's how I like it. No responsibility, no worries, just a basic life. Mind you, it wouldn't be possible if I had to pay for camping every night, so this place is a real lifesaver."

"And you hung out with Ben a lot?"

"Sure. Saw him around all the time. We'd get together when we were in the mood. Have a drink, sometimes cook together. Sit around a fire nattering about this and that. He was a good guy. Complicated, annoying as hell sometimes, but a decent man. What was the killer like, Max?"

I explained what little I'd managed to see before being hit, and Russell listened in silence, occasionally nodding his head. Tilly glanced at him repeatedly, as if waiting for something, but when I'd finished he was silent, stroking his chin, the rasp of his stubble and the jangle of his chains around his neck the only sound.

"Do you have something to say, Russell?" asked Tilly.

"His past caught up with him."

"Meaning?" I asked.

"Meaning, Ben was a downright liar, although never a cheat, but underneath it all he was an honest man. We didn't serve together, but I know a soldier when I see one."

"You served?"

"For longer than I'd liked. At least, it felt like that sometimes when I was out there in some nasty places. I toured all over in my twenties and into my mid-thirties, but it's a young man's game. It began to get too much. The things I saw, the things I did, they took their toll. Not to mention how hard it is on the body. I was a grunt, just a soldier, but I could tell Ben was more than that."

"Like what?" asked Tilly.

"Special ops would be my guess. SAS or something similar. Maybe something even more covert."

"He never talked about it with you?"

"Never. And if you knew Ben, that wasn't like him at all. Everyone around here knows he was in the army, he was always telling people, but you won't find a soul who heard him tell a story about it, even an outlandish one."

"He's right, Max. Ben was a real talker, but never about his past. Just nonsense about new vans and what he'd been up to."

"We talked a lot over the years, and I asked a few

times, but never pushed it. He had this way about him though. There was something in how he did things, even how he moved, the things he knew, that made me certain he was much more than he seemed. Most likely, he did something in the army that pushed him over the edge and made him jack it in. He was definitely traumatised. I know I am." Russell laughed, then sank his pint, a sad, faraway look in his eyes. "Some of us can't cope after what we saw and did, you know? It gets to you. Normal life seems so, well, normal after that. At least camping, or living in a van, and roaming around the area gives you an edge to hold on to. Makes life interesting enough to bother facing another day."

"But why would someone come after him now?" I wondered. "It's been so long. He's been around here for fifteen years hasn't he?"

"Sounds about right."

"That's a long time for someone to hold a grudge."

"Or a long time for someone to find him. Maybe Ben isn't even his real name. Maybe he was in witness protection but left, or maybe he was just plain hiding from someone. Who knows? But by the sounds of it, the man who did for him was a soldier."

"Or wanted to look like one. Russell, I really appreciate you talking to us, but are you certain? Could Ben have made up the whole army thing, and the truth is he was a loner who wanted a simple life like you? A drifter? I can see your reasoning, but you said it yourself he was a terrible liar."

"Anything's possible, Max, but I don't think so. I might not know much about Ben, but one thing I do know is that he was ex-military. I'd bet my life on it." Russell stood, nodded, and said, "Right, I have an appointment with the sea. Time for my afternoon swim."

After he'd left, I asked Tilly, "Is he on the level? He's not like Ben, is he?"

"Russell grew up in Harlech, lived in Barmouth for ages, but now mostly stays on the campsite or a few other local spots where he knows people and doesn't have to pay."

"And he was a soldier. That's confirmed?"

"Max, don't be so suspicious! Yes, he's legit. He has family in the area, his folks are still alive. Neighbours, friends, all of that. He's on the level. He was a soldier for many years, but wasn't right when he returned. Couldn't settle. He's happy now. Where he belongs."

"And he's certain Ben was some kind of covert operative before he turned up here fifteen years ago?"

"Sounds like it. Russell's a very good judge of character and a super nice guy. He's smart, and likeable, but very down to earth. He looked out for Ben. Think he's right? That this was to do with his past?"

"I'm not sure. It's the obvious explanation, but that doesn't mean it's the right one. Let me think about it." I turned at the sound of Tilly's name being called and readied myself for what was to come. A long line of police vehicles and an ambulance were queued at the entrance, so Tilly nodded to me then rushed over to deal with them.

Knowing it was best to get this over with sooner rather than later, I stayed where I was and finished my drink while Tilly helped arrange for the vehicles to either park or drive down to Ben's van. The ambulance and several police cars, along with a handful of unmarked vehicles, drove straight down, while a few parked and several officers emerged. They spoke to Tilly first, which I assumed would take a while, so it gave me time to mull over what Russell had said.

My first question was could I trust him? I wasn't sure. There was something about the limp, and how casual yet made-to-be-obvious it was that gave me pause. Maybe I shouldn't have watched The Usual Suspects as now I was almost convinced we had a Keyser Söze in our midst! Could Russell be responsible? Maybe he was telling the truth about being a soldier and it was him who had a grudge against Ben. But he'd lived in the area his whole life, so wasn't exactly hunting down Ben, was he? And if he was the killer, why try to convince us Ben was on the level about being in the army and go into so much detail about what the most likely reason for Ben's murder was?

I was barking up the wrong tree. At this rate I'd be suspecting Tilly next!

Could she? Would she? Maybe she didn't like him as much as she'd said. Maybe there had been issues. Unwanted advances, something more sinister? No, it had been a man, right? Thinking back on it, and picturing the approaching killer, was I so sure it was a man? Average height and build, not exactly muscular, with more of a wiry frame, but that was all I'd seen. The killer was covered up in cargo trousers, boots, a black hoodie, a balaclava, and the hood pulled over their head for good measure. I was merely going on the way they moved, but could I be mistaken?

There was no time for more of my ridiculous musings as a cough caused me to look up and find two officers standing in front of me.

They asked if they could take a statement, both rather cautious and almost in awe, then they explained that I was the talk of the station, along with Ben's murder of course, and they couldn't believe they got to talk to me. I thanked them politely, offered for them to sit, then spent the next hour going over my story and getting chastised for hot-wiring a van—I told them I did it so Dad wouldn't be in trouble—and digging up a corpse.

They were going through the motions, though, and clearly weren't concerned about what I'd done. Their focus was on what I would do next, even after I explained that I'd been warned off by the detectives and told to go for a long walk on the beach while they investigated.

Both agreed that was for the best, but were clearly keen to know what I thought of the whole incident, and asked if it was true what'd happened to me yesterday. They'd spoken to the officers I'd given my statement to, but wanted to hear it from me. So I had to go over that story again, too, until they were satisfied, then once they'd rather sheepishly asked for an autograph, which I gave with a smile even though it felt beyond weird and not quite right, they told me that was it and I could leave.

I was absolutely not to interfere, though, or go near the van today. They would be in a lot of trouble, and so would I, so I promised to steer clear and just enjoy a walk, cook dinner, and stay at my pitch. They said there was no need to talk to my folks, which was a relief, so once they'd left, I finished my pint then drove back to our pitch to find Mum, Dad, and Anxious fast asleep and curled up on the rug under the gazebo.

Rather than wake them, I took a seat and let the day's events play out until I had everything in some kind of order. It had been a very strange and trying time and I was exhausted, but knew I couldn't sleep yet. When Anxious woke up, I quietly retrieved his lead, shook it at him so he wagged, and left a note for my folks before we headed off towards the west and the long sandy beach according to the map.

The walk did me good and cleared my head of the booze fog, leaving me free to enjoy my time alone with Anxious. He was in his element, chasing imaginary rabbits, following scent trails, bounding up and down the dunes before we emerged onto a road that took us directly to the beach. We cut off across a narrow track through the dunes, then emerged onto a glorious stretch of pristine beach with the water at high tide.

We raced down to the shore and I slipped off my Crocs then paddled in the shallows with Anxious trotting about and having the best time ever.

Sometimes I found it hard to believe quite how beautiful this country was. Why would I ever want to go abroad again?

Tapas?

Chapter 8

Clearly, more people were interested in the beach than crabbing. It was large enough to accommodate everyone and most likely hundreds more without it being cramped, but it was obviously a hotspot for those on the island. Unlike so many beaches in Devon and Cornwall, nobody had to sit right next to anyone else, making it about as enjoyable as a sun lounger at the side of a swimming pool on a Bank Holiday Monday. Here, everyone had as much room as they wished, especially once you got away from the parking areas.

Anxious and I were in our element, enjoying each other's company and just walking and talking like the best friends we were. Sure, the conversation was rather one-sided, but that didn't bother either him or me. This was why the company of a dog was such a beautiful thing. You always had a buddy, and someone who would listen without judgement. A pure, entirely innocent devotion and love that could calm the most unsettled of minds and lift you from your darkest moments.

I'd lost track of how many times Anxious had drawn me out of a funk, or forced me to go for a walk when all I wanted to do was stay put and feel sorry for myself. No matter what your mood, dogs still needed walking, feeding, and caring for. It brought you out of yourself and made you tend to them, and that was a good thing.

Halfway along the massive stretch of beach, I spied

the man from the bar who'd served us. What was his name? Tony? He was talking to another man, a slim guy with faded tattoos over his arms, a wiry frame, short hair clipped almost to the bone, and a ramrod straight back. The conversation was clearly animated as they were both waving their arms around before moving closer and getting right up in each other's faces.

Several people wandered past and said hello to Tony. Those who had been coming here for years, I assumed, and knew all the staff. Tony replied with a smile, but the moment they were alone they began arguing again. Nobody spoke to the other man, so I assumed he was a stranger and not a staff member.

Anxious and I did our best to stay out of sight, not easy on a beach, but we remained by the water beside a large group and I just watched as best I could.

The man pointed up into the dunes, then marched off in that direction. Tony followed behind a few seconds later, not trying to catch up but keeping the mystery man in sight.

"Should we follow them?"

Anxious was up for it, or at least the walk, so keeping well back and using the other visitors as a way to mask us, we trailed behind. Tony stopped and turned at the dunes, but we'd lucked out and were right behind a family, so when I peeked Tony was already at the ridge then vanished.

Warning Anxious to remain close, as we didn't want a repeat of yesterday, and my nerves certainly couldn't handle it, we climbed the steep bank. I got onto all fours and peered over the edge down into the sand dunes proper that stretched right up to a road and east to west for seemingly miles.

But I wasn't here to admire the flora and fauna. I was here to see if I could catch a killer. There was nobody in sight, so I slid down the other side and cautiously began to search the area, listening for any sounds, mindful of the attack yesterday. I was nervous, and brave enough to admit it. Why wouldn't I be? I didn't want to end up like Ben, so should I even be doing this? Jittery and having to remind Anxious repeatedly not to stray even though he hadn't, I put him on the lead just to be sure, although he couldn't understand why.

A noise made me stop dead in my tracks, then duck down behind a clump of spiky grass. We poked our heads out and saw Russell walking past, carrying a heavy rucksack, and I almost called out a warning but something stopped me just as I opened my mouth. Was he going to see the others? Out for a stroll? Up to something on his own? Maybe he was heading to the beach for another swim? It didn't look like it as he wasn't angling towards the water, but he might know of a spot further along the coast.

With my ears primed for any noise, a dull thud just over the next dune made me decide on my next course of action and I raced down, almost falling, then scrambled up the other side and slid down again. There in the bowl of the dunes, protected on all sides from prying eyes unless you were really unlucky, was Russell. I hurried over, my fears forgotten, and skidded onto my knees in the sand next to the ex-soldier.

Russell was on his back, his rucksack making his flat stomach arc high and stretch out his ribcage through his green vest. One leg was at an unnatural angle where it had twisted as he'd fallen, the shin at a right angle to the thigh, and clearly broken. It didn't matter, and would never be repaired, as a bullet hole through his forehead meant he would never stay another night on the island. His face was turned to the side, his eyes staring right at me, and as I crawled close I gasped as I'd got an answer for Mum as to whether the bullet would come out the back of the head. It most certainly would, and it had made a terrible mess in the sand.

Gagging, I sank back and sat, dazed, confused, and a little scared. Anxious whined and shifted onto my lap then licked my cheek, telling me it was okay and not to be scared. I cuddled him tight, but only for a moment, then I jumped up and ran up the dune away from the beach and spied Tony and the other man walking away from the scene fast.

Checking my phone, I cursed the lack of a signal yet again, but then it sprang into life and I quickly called reception hoping Tilly would answer. I told her what had happened, asked if the police were still there and they were, so she promised to tell them immediately and would show them the way after I did my best to explain.

The wait was one of the longest of my life.

Every sound, every time the grass blew in the wind, every shift of the sand or small insect that hopped from the ground made my heart leap and my pulse quicken.

Finally, voices could be heard, and I made out Tilly telling someone where I was, so stood and climbed the dune then waved at her and three officers, two who had questioned me earlier. They hurried over, but when they arrived I told Tilly she should stay back, and to be careful, then showed the officers the body.

They checked he was dead, which he obviously was, then set up a cordon before ushering me over to Tilly who was ashen.

"I'm so sorry. I saw Tony from the bar arguing with another man and thought it might have been important. They came this way, then I saw Russell. Next thing I knew, he was dead and I saw Tony and the other guy hurrying off."

"What is going on around here?" gasped Tilly, eyes drifting to the body and the officer calling it in on his radio.

"It seems like someone's out to murder ex-soldiers."

"That's a good hypothesis," said the officer, grinning at me.

"Everyone said he was good," agreed the other. "Can we get a statement please?"

"Another one?" I sighed, wishing I'd stayed with Mum and Dad and had a nap.

"Afraid so. Don't worry, it won't take long. Wow, a double murder."

"And of two people I thought highly of," snapped Tilly, frowning at their keen faces.

"Yes, sorry. It's just nothing like this ever happens around here."

Tilly waited while I gave an official statement, then we were told we could go but to be careful. I wondered if the officers knew what they were doing, as surely we shouldn't be alone? I still got out of there as fast as possible, as much for her sake as mine. She was upset, and kept repeating herself, saying it didn't seem real, and why would anyone do it, but I had no answers for her.

I walked with her right back to the reception, where we stopped in the car park and watched Tony being bundled into a police car. There was no sign of the other man, but Tilly went and checked and apparently he'd already been taken away as they'd come back to the bar together.

"Is that it?" she asked when she returned.

"Maybe. If it was them. Do you know Tony well?"

"I know everyone who works here. He's always behind the bar, but likes to walk on the beach when it's his break or his shift is over, and he's always been lovely. He's not the type to murder anyone, and besides, did they have a gun?"

"Not that I could see. There was nowhere to hide one that I could tell. Not a rifle, anyway. Maybe it was a simple handgun. You can hide one of those easily."

"Max, this doesn't ring true at all. Tony isn't the type. He's mild-mannered and always happy. He didn't even know Ben and Russell like I did. He keeps to himself even though he's chatty and polite with the customers."

"Let's see what the police find out and take it from there. But my advice is to be careful and not wander around alone. Are you going to be okay?"

"Yes, fine thanks. My shift just finished, so I'm going to go right home, lock the doors, and pour myself a generous glass of wine. You take care, too, Max. We're a part of this now, so keep an eye out and don't do anything rash."

"I won't. Thanks for your help again."

"My pleasure. Um, not pleasure. You know what I mean!" Tilly wiped her eyes, smiled sadly at me, then hurried back to the reception building, presumably to get her things.

Anxious and I made the long trek back to base camp, the now familiar roads and tracks taking on a sinister edge because of the numerous switchbacks where someone could be lurking, ready to pounce and claim me as the next victim if it turned out that Tony and his acquaintance weren't the killer or killers. I didn't know what to think, and neither did Anxious, who had already forgotten about the mad stuff humans got up to and was delighting in yet another walk.

For me, I was totally over it, and fed up with the repetition of going back and forth after one disaster led to another.

As we approached, I stopped and sighed. "I forgot to call Mum and Dad. They'll be really worried. We've been gone for ages. They'll be going spare."

Anxious cocked his head and licked his nose, then whined in agreement. We knew what Mum could be like once she got a bee in her bonnet.

Just before the last turn onto the small track, the grubby old quad trundled past, the back full of maintenance equipment like brushes and shovels, a chainsaw, large bags of rubbish, stacks of firewood, and tarps covering who knew what. The driver turned as he drove past, the helmet making it impossible to see if they were smiling or frowning. I nodded, and the driver lifted a hand in recognition, then was past me, presumably continuing the endless round of maintenance and deliveries working on such a large site would entail.

There was no time to study him more as the quad sped up, kicking sand at us as it skidded on the road then was gone. I was too tired to even care by now, and just wanted to sit, have a drink, then potter in the kitchen and make dinner.

Dreading Mum's ire almost as much as a potential attack, I couldn't believe my eyes when we arrived back at the pitch. They hadn't moved a muscle. My note was where I'd left it, and the pair were still fast asleep and snoring. I checked my watch and noted it must have been almost three hours since I'd first gone up to get help after we found Ben, and they were still out of it.

I guess they really hadn't had any sleep the night before thanks to Anxious hogging the bed and them worrying about me, but even by their standards it was pushing things too far. Still, I was relieved, as it meant I could sit in my chair, drink a cold, lovely fizzy glass of Prosecco, and not have to explain anything to anyone.

Not dealing with a detective felt strange, but part of me understood why they wanted to keep their distance, the other part surprised as surely they knew my reputation and that I'd poke my nose in. Especially now I'd found the second corpse. Russell had seemed like a nice guy, too, and was well-respected around here, so I'd have assumed the detective would want to hear every detail. But there wasn't that much to tell, and I had explained to the officers, so maybe whoever was running this really didn't want the extra hassle of having to deal with me too.

It still didn't feel right. Something was going on. This wasn't how investigations were run. At least, none I'd been involved in. The detectives always wanted to talk to those involved, even if statements were taken by officers. It was the way things were done, and how they got as full a picture of events as possible.

Slowly, I began to unwind, and as it grew rather cool under the gazebo I scooted forward into the sunshine. As my pulse slowed, so I sipped my wine and began to enjoy the late afternoon peace. With nothing but the sound of my family snoring, Anxious already having squeezed between my folks and curled up upside down, legs akimbo, I was finally allowed some private time where nothing happened, nobody died, no suspicious activity occurred, and for once I wasn't pestered by the police or having to deal with a grumpy detective warning me off the case.

As I reached for the bottle to have a second glass, Mum and Dad slowly began to stir. It began with a grunt, then a mumble, so I turned to enjoy the show, tittering into my hand as I watched the nutty ones' unique way of waking from an extended nap.

Mum slapped an arm out which almost flattened Anxious but luckily whacked onto Dad's belly. He swatted it away with a grunt, then rolled over, now facing Anxious. Not missing the opportunity, he licked Dad's nose, which made Dad rub at it. While this was going on, Mum's leg twitched, then shot out sideways, booting Dad in the shin with the point of her heel. He rolled over the other way, so Anxious turned his attention to Mum and licked her cheek, which made her rub at it.

Meanwhile, Dad was slowly coming around, so scratched at his chin, then his hand lowered and sank beneath the front of his jeans, which was when I decided I'd had enough. As I was about to turn, Mum shot upright, shrieked, and Dad sprang to standing in a flash, a fighting stance assumed, scanning in all directions as he shouted, "I'll have you, you buggers. Leave my wife alone!"

"What's going on?" shouted Mum, rubbing at her eyes.

Anxious barked, then jumped up, unsure what was happening.

"It's okay. Everyone calm down. Mum, you woke Dad, and he jumped to your defence like the gallant hero he is."

"Aw, thanks, love," cooed Mum, checking her dress then standing with the help of Dad.

They embraced, and kissed, then turned to me and Dad asked, "So there's no attacker?"

"Nobody here but us."

"I thought you were going up to reception to get help for poor Ben? Shouldn't you be doing that?" asked Mum, wagging a finger. "Not sitting there drinking all the wine. You better have saved some for us."

"There's plenty more in the fridge, and I did go to

get help. You two fell asleep."

"Only for a quick forty winks," said Dad.

"More like three hours. After the police came, I gave a statement, then I came back and you were sleeping. We went to the beach, I found a guy I met earlier dead, dealt with the cops again, then have been sitting here drinking for a while."

"He's such a character," laughed Dad.

"A real joker at times," agreed Mum with a happy smile. "Max, you shouldn't tease us like that."

"I'm not. It's true. I'll tell you all about it, but let me fix you both a drink first."

Once we'd settled, I started at the beginning, knowing this would not be quick, but trying my best to rush through it so I could get dinner on. The moment I began my tale, I knew it would be a very late meal, and I wasn't wrong.

Chapter 9

I ended up having to begin preparing dinner whilst still recounting the tale. If I hadn't, it would have been midnight before we'd eaten. My excited parents wanted to know every single detail and kept making me repeat everything at least three times. I wondered if they needed hearing aids, but had to remind myself that they'd always been like this—once they got into something they wanted as clear a picture as possible. Plus, and this was the most important thing, they loved to natter.

Both gave their opinion, multiple times, about why the men were killed and who might be responsible, finally settling on it being Tony the barman, possibly with the man he'd argued with as an accomplice. With both now being questioned at the station, I guessed we'd find out the next day what the deal was, but I had my doubts. It was too obvious, but maybe that was the point. Maybe there was something in Ben's past, possibly Russell's, too, that meant Tony had it in for them. A long-lost son of one man? Maybe Russell was the real reason Ben was killed. A case of mistaken identity? Or maybe Tony's father or the other man's had served with one of the men and this was payback for something that went wrong back in their army days?

It was all conjecture, of course, but that didn't stop us all from speculating, the ideas getting wilder the more wine Mum and Dad drank and the more excited we got as dinnertime approached.

Keeping it simple, I'd gone for a one-pot burrito, if you discounted the frying pan for heating up the tortillas. And this was the secret to a great burrito, I'd discovered after years of trial and error. Don't over-complicate the filling, try to use as few pans as possible, and spend money on the best possible tortillas. As my folks finally settled into a companionable silence, praise be, I thought back on the numerous arguments I'd had with fellow chefs over what constituted the perfect burrito.

Having worked with Mexicans, a Texan, a foul-mouthed woman from California, an Italian, and chefs from just about every country you could think of, there were endless opinions on what should go inside, what tortillas to use, how long to warm them, even arguments so heated they once resulted in a fight when two Mexicans got into a heated discussion about the chilli level and whether the beans should be re-fried or kept whole.

My perfect burrito was the culmination of years of working as a chef making fancy food where such simple fare was never on the menu, but during breaks, or lulls in service, conversation often turned to so-called "peasant food" like this. It had become a running joke around the restaurants as everyone compared recipes, the arguments sometimes raucous, but mostly good-natured and a welcome break from the serious business of fancy restaurant food.

I had to modify my approach to accommodate one-pot cooking, but less than you'd think. Rice was cooked first in my trusty cast-iron pot, a strict ten minutes on a low heat then ten off, the lid always on to stop the steam escaping. Once done, I emptied out the rice, fried off the chicken I'd flattened with a rolling pin, then set about the rest. Once ready, and it truly was a fast dish to make, it all went back in the pot to reheat while I got Dad involved by heating the tortillas on the rack over the small fire he and Mum had made, their bickering about how to build a fire the best way something they never seemed to tire of getting into.

Mum was always the same whenever Dad or I built a fire or did barbecue when I was growing up. Even though

Dad was a whizz with the charcoal, and had been doing it for decades, she always had an opinion on how it should be done, never mind the fact she would never go near a lump of charcoal for fear of getting her hands, or even worse, her dress, dirty.

The background noise of their loving arguing made me smile, and stopped me dwelling on the deaths that had marred my stay here so far. I'd been here for a day and a night and already found two dead men, been hospitalised, and had my best friend kidnapped. Yet standing here, dishing up the burrito mix into a bowl and sorting out yoghurt, coriander, and the rest of the accompaniments, it faded, the stress lifted, and I wallowed in the company of my family.

Dad ignored Mum's insistence on letting the tortillas brown, which they shouldn't, and handed me the plate stacked high. I loaded them up, folded them how they were meant to be folded—there is only one correct way, all chefs and street vendors agree on at least that one point—then served my eager folks who were seated in their chairs and on their best behaviour as their focus turned to food.

Anxious had his own special burrito without kidney beans or onion or garlic, meaning chicken and rice and the tortilla, so we all tucked in, the first bite of succulent, heavily spiced chicken combined with the cheese, sour yoghurt, herbs, and mushy beans a delight as always.

Although large, everyone wanted a second, so I did the honours and we slowly worked our way through them, chatting about regular things, sipping freezing cold wine from the coolbox, and enjoying the fire that crackled pleasantly on a lovely mild evening in the sand dunes, content to be in such fine company. Our own little oasis amidst a mad world that sometimes felt like it could overwhelm us and make a mockery of all we held dear in this world. But we wouldn't let it. We were strong as a family, much stronger than as individuals, and we knew it.

After I'd cleaned up the kitchen, giving me a few minutes of alone time while my folks relaxed by the fire, I joined them, warming my hands after the lukewarm water from the dishes.

"Max, you should come with us. It's too dangerous to stay here. What if the killer strikes again?" Mum wrung her hands, no easy job as she refused to let go of her wine glass.

"She's right, Son. This places is a deathtrap. You've been clobbered, Anxious got nicked, two blokes were shot in the head, and you were hospitalised. Nasty business."

Mum nodded vigorously, then sipped her wine, never taking her eyes off me.

"I'll be fine. Nobody's out to get me. I was just in the wrong place at the wrong time."

"More like the wrong time at the right place," said Mum, nodding to herself then raising an eyebrow as she waited for us to agree.

"I have no idea what that means," I said, shaking my head, wondering about this crazy woman and what might go on in her head.

"Me either." Dad glanced quickly at her then changed his mind and said, "Yes, nice one, love. Well said."

"See, your father agrees." Mum smiled smugly, then turned serious and said, "Really, Max, you should leave with us."

"Where are you staying anyway? You've both had wine, so you can't drive. It's a long walk to any hotels."

"Aha, they have a little cottage, so we rented that. We lucked out as they had a last-minute cancellation. We would have stayed there last night, but didn't want to upset Anxious. He was more at home in Vee."

"So you aren't even leaving anyway! You'll be on the island too."

"Yes, but that's different," said Dad. "We'll have solid walls and locks and a proper bedroom."

"Plus a bathroom," boasted Mum, winking. "Tempting, eh? Proper bathroom, with a hot shower, a flushing loo, and all the soap you will ever need."

"I have soap!"

"Yes, but no toilet or shower," grumbled Mum, tutting. "Max, come stay with us."

"Thanks for the offer, but I want to stay here. I was away yesterday, and it's been such a long day with finding two bodies. I want something familiar, and Vee is my home. I know you both mean well, but honestly we'll be fine. Anxious won't let anything happen, will you, boy?"

We turned to him, and I was really hoping for some backup here, but the little guy was on his side, fast asleep, legs twitching as he chased rabbits in his dreams.

"I guess the little soldier will look after you," Dad conceded. "But make sure to lock the van, and don't let anyone in if they knock."

"Who would knock?"

"How should I know? A man with a rifle, wanting to execute you?"

Mum gasped, eyes wide, and emergency adjusted her bandanna.

"Now look what you've done! You upset your mother. It's alright, love, Max won't get shot in the head in the night, will you, Max?"

"I'll try not to. And I didn't upset her, you did."

"Me? What did I say?"

"That I'd get shot in the head."

"Will you both stop talking about it!" Mum dabbed at her eyes delicately so as not to mess up her make-up, then stood, ruffled out her dress so it hung nicely, clicked her heels together, and said, "Max, thank you for a lovely dinner, and for putting up with us silly old fools. I know you'll be fine, but we do worry. It's dangerous here, although very beautiful, and let's not pretend otherwise. You were attacked, so was Anxious, and in the middle of the day. Be careful, and don't open the van for strangers."

"I promise I won't. Please don't worry. Whatever is going on here, it isn't me they're after. It's something else. I just don't know what yet."

"You'll figure it out. You always do." Dad slapped me on the back then pulled me in for a hug, the smell of his aftershave and Brylcreem soothing me, the familiarity of it making me feel like a child again.

"Thanks. Look after Mum."

"I will. Same as always."

"Hey, stop hogging our boy!" Mum shoved Dad aside and cuddled me tight, fighting back her tears.

"I'll be fine, Mum. You look after Dad, okay?" I winked at Dad over the top of her head, and he nodded with a smile.

"Of course I will. I always have and I always will." Mum pulled away, looked into my eyes, and smiled before kissing my cheek.

"I'll walk with you anyway, so no need to say goodnight just yet." I bent to Anxious and shook him gently, then asked if he fancied a walk to take Jack and Jill to their cottage. He yawned, then was up and raring to go. I always marvelled at how quickly he could go from comatose to full of energy, and it brought a smile to my face same as always.

Mum lamented not being able to take all their things to the cottage, but a few glasses of wine meant it was out of the question. Driving around late at night on narrow tracks where people were in tents either side was a recipe for disaster. It was dangerous enough with Dad behind the wheel during the daytime and totally sober, let alone now it was dark.

The walk ended up being fun anyway. Mum would have to wait until the morning for her stuff, but Dad still got lumbered with several kilos worth of make-up, a clean dress, and who knew what else Mum forced into a huge backpack much to her disgust as she insisted her dress should be hung on a hanger, not treated like an army vest.

The site had quietened down from the early evening, but several spots were clearly party groups out for a good time, and I was glad I hadn't stayed in any of the large fields. Sleep would be nigh on impossible with a group of ten drinking and playing music late into the night, and I wondered if they'd get told to quiet down by the staff or if everyone was left to it undisturbed.

Other pitches were much calmer with couples or lone campers sitting outside by fires or late barbecues, poking at the coals and sipping drinks, the atmosphere sedate and almost dreamy. I loved wandering around campsites at this time of the evening. It was magical, with all the low voices, the fires, the smell of smoke and burnt burgers, zips opening and closing. Nearly everyone had a string of fairy lights or a lantern hanging from a handy hook, creating little pockets of intimacy around their lodgings, long shadows cast over their faces as they chatted quietly or simply stared into the flames and soaked up the freedom, the chance to get away from routines, avoid technology, and get back to nature.

Of course, there were plenty of people still glued to their phones, oblivious to what was all around them, and I wished they would just put them away and allow themselves the luxury of being bored, of simply sitting and doing nothing, but I knew how hard that was to do when trips away were few and far between. It was the one definite difference I'd noted over the last nine or ten months. Vanlifers, or those who went away camping or in their vans on a regular basis, were much less likely to be addicted to tech gadgets. That didn't mean we weren't obsessed by the gear now available—it sometimes felt like a challenge to see who could find the smallest possible gas burner or the most compact collapsible fire bowl.

The more you spent time outdoors, the more you did away with the tech, though, and the closer you felt to nature. People were happy to sit and do nothing, to take note of what was happening around them, admire the scenery, listen to the wind and the birds, raise their heads to the sun, revel in the feel of grass or damp sand between their toes. It crept up on everyone slowly, but without exception those who spent more time away from screens did so because they'd gradually realised getting back to basics was much more rewarding and less stressful.

So I couldn't help chuckling to myself when I caught

my folks up and found them both staring at their phones as they walked like zombies. I had to steer them back onto the path before they flattened a poor guy's tent.

"Careful where you're going. What are you both doing staring at your phones? That isn't like you."

"I have to update the wiki page," said Dad, tapping away.

"And I have to correct his spelling. Jack always rushes things so I check for typos."

"And tell me exactly what to write, even though I ignore your mother as I'm the creative one and it's my page anyway."

"It is not! I help lots, and you use half the things I say to put on there. Oh, that was a good bit, Jack." Mum kissed Dad's cheek, making him puff out his chest.

"You think? I thought it worked well too. All the fans will love this."

"Fans? What fans? This is the first I'm hearing about fans. It's a wiki page about the cases I'm involved in, although you do share too much personal information, Dad."

"It gives a fuller picture of what's going on. People like to know intimate details."

"And who are these people?"

"Everyone who gets in touch with your father to discuss your cases. They have a forum now. It's linked on the wiki page."

"You talk about me? To strangers? Dad, that's not cool."

"Course it is. People want to know."

"And I bet you tell them, don't you?" I sighed.

"Nothing private," he protested.

"Well, apart from what's going on with him and Min. And how Anxious is. Sometimes you chat with them about Max's fussy behaviour, and if it's normal to be so obsessed with cleaning the kitchen and having those stackable plastic boxes," said Mum helpfully, causing Dad to splutter and cough.

"Yes, er, sometimes, but like I said, nothing personal."

"Dad! What are you thinking?"

Mum and Dad both stopped, lowered their phones, and together chorused, "We're proud of you. We like to tell people."

"I know, and I appreciate it, but it feels like I'm always being watched. Judged. It's all got so strange. People know me when I go places. I don't like it. I want my privacy."

"Son, we know you're a private person, and that's fine, but you do important work and you've helped so many over this past year that we want everyone to know. Did we do a bad thing?" Dad frowned, clearly uncomfortable, which was a first.

"No, it's fine. I guess this has got me shaken up and I'm antsy. Tomorrow will be better. Maybe it's the lack of police around, the fact the site is running like normal, and not talking to the detective in charge. I don't even know who it is."

Dad smiled smugly. "I do."

"How?"

"Someone on the forum knows the brother of the wife of the next-door neighbour of…"

I zoned out for a while, and came to with my folks right in my face, peering at me. "What's wrong?"

"You were off on one of your daydreams again," said Mum. "Time for bed for you. You always get like this when you're tired. And we're here."

"I am a grown man. I choose my own bedtime," I said with a smile, knowing it would always be like this.

"Of course." Mum kissed me, Dad and I hugged, then they said goodnight to us and I waited until I heard the door lock.

Anxious and I returned to Vee in companionable silence, just the quiet murmurs of campers and the rip of zips as people settled for the night.

    I could barely keep my eyes open as I sorted things back at Vee, and Anxious and I were asleep five minutes later.

Chapter 10

Something wasn't right, but I didn't know what. I didn't exactly jump out of bed and race to the window, but I did sit up and flick the light on. It didn't blind me, but allowed me to see enough to know that it was still just us guys inside Vee.

I turned to Anxious, surprised to find him awake. He was sitting up, ears twitching, eyes locked on the door.

I strained to hear, and thought maybe footsteps were approaching, but it could have been my understandably very active imagination.

Anxious whined quietly, but remained motionless.

Someone hammered on the door. I jumped a mile as my bodyguard leapt from the bed onto the tiny patch of free floor space and began barking, his hackles raised.

What should I do? Open up? Shout out? Pray for a phone signal and call the cops? Grab one of my knives?

"Max, it's me, Tilly. Are you in there? Anxious, don't bark, and don't be afraid. I want to talk to Max."

I sighed with relief, but then began to stress about Tilly being the killer and what if she'd come to finish me off in the night? She was a nice woman, and had been very helpful, but what if I was wrong? She was tall enough to have been the gunman, and always seemed to be around when things went wrong, so what if? I gave myself a stern talking to, as of course she was always around as I went to tell her. She couldn't be at reception and off whacking ex-soldiers simultaneously, now could she?

Feeling suitably sheepish, I called out, "I'm here. Give me a moment." I checked the time. Half one. What was she doing here?

I slipped on my shorts and vest, then unlocked the van door and opened up, shocked by her appearance.

"Sorry it's so late, but I figured you'd want to know."

"Know what? Are you alright? You don't look the best. Come in. Um, scrap that, there's no room. I'll come out."

"Okay. Sorry again." Tilly took a few steps back, her hair all over the place now it wasn't tied back, her face rather red, wearing nothing but a pair of shorts and a grey cardigan she kept hugging around herself as her eyes darted constantly like she was worried someone was coming.

"What's going on?" I stepped down and checked we were alone, her nervous behaviour making me edgy.

"I know it's late, but I had to come and tell you. And if I look a mess, it's because I got dragged in to working late dealing with all the police, then had a few drinks in the bar as we have a lock-in sometimes, and then we heard so I thought I should come and tell you."

"Whoa, slow down. Take it from the beginning. What's happened?"

"They released Tony and the guy he was with."

"Who told you?"

"I heard one of the cops talking. They left two young officers up at the entrance, just to be sure, and we got chatting. One had a call and was told Tony was free to return to work. Not that he did tonight, obviously, but he'll be back tomorrow."

"Okay, so that's good, isn't it? The police believe he's innocent. Who was the other man?"

"Just a friend of his, apparently. They bumped into each other on the beach. I told you Tony likes to take a walk on his break or when his shift is over."

"You did, yes. Um, Tilly, why are you really here? Couldn't this have waited until the morning? And should you be wandering around the site at this time?"

"I got nervous, worried about Tony and this other guy, but felt silly. Everyone else said it obviously wasn't him as we all like Tony and he's never any bother, but I guess I wanted someone to talk to who doesn't work here and is involved. They don't get how stressful this has been."

"I know it's hard, but you have to try and relax. You like Tony and said he's always been friendly. If he was questioned, then released, I'm sure that's because he's innocent."

"Max, I don't know what to think!" Tilly tugged at the stretched sleeves of the cardigan then crossed her arms and shivered. "Everything's just awful. Russell was killed yesterday. Murdered. And you found him. And before that, poor Ben. He was my friend, the stupid, lying idiot. I liked them both. Now they're gone. I feel like I'm losing my mind."

"It's the stress. I get it. Your mind's working overtime trying to deal with it. I'm sorry I put so much of this on you. Dealing with the police and all the other teams is a lot to cope with. It will be different in the morning, you'll see. Want to sit for a while?" I indicated the chairs and she nodded.

I grabbed a half-finished bottle of wine from the coolbox and some glasses then joined her.

Anxious curled up between us, unsure what was going on, but too tired to care.

I handed Tilly her drink and she smiled then took a sip. "Thanks."

"You were with friends, so why come and see me?"

"Because you're the only one who understands. You were there, and have dealt with this kind of thing before. It's overwhelming, and so sad. Everyone else who works here doesn't feel the same. They're upset, and worried, sure, but not like if they'd been a part of it. I'm being silly, aren't I?"

"Not at all. Apart from me, you're closest to this, and

with the worry about Tony being involved, it's a lot to handle. What were you told about him being let out?"

"That he had an alibi for Ben's murder. He was working, and was in the bar when you were attacked, so it couldn't have been him. I don't know about the other guy, but I guess the police are happy enough if they released them both."

"There you go then. Nothing to worry about."

"Nothing to worry about!?" Tilly laughed manically, drained her wine, then looked me in the eye and said, "Two ex-soldiers were shot in the head. That is most definitely something to worry about. Aren't you stressed or concerned?"

"Sure, a little, but whatever this is about, I don't think it's me, and certainly not you, who they're after. There's a reason for this, and I intend to find out."

"But what reason? And how can you be sure?"

"Just a feeling. I've been doing this long enough now to go with my gut instinct, and that's telling me that this is something that goes back a long way. I was in the wrong place so got involved, but that's it. You certainly don't need to worry."

"The killer is still on the loose though. It could be anyone and he could be anywhere." Tilly snatched up the wine and emptied the bottle into her glass, seemingly oblivious.

"Or they're long gone. Tilly, there is nothing for you to worry about. Nobody is after you. Even if they're still here, they won't hurt you. Why would they?"

"Because I'm involved, like you. Everyone knows that I called the police and was friends with them both. And they know I'm a nosy so-and-so and won't let this lie until I get justice. You will help find the killer, Max, won't you?"

"Of course I will. I already told you that."

"Yes, sorry. I'm a bag of nerves. This isn't like me. Normally, I'm cool under pressure and can handle anything."

"Come on, let me walk you back. Where do you live? Not on site?"

"Sometimes I stay here, and tonight I definitely am. There are rooms in the pub and a few are staying there for an early shift, so I'll nab a free one and try to get some sleep. Max, I apologise. I woke you and stole all your wine." With a cheesy grin, Tilly gulped her full glass then wiped her mouth.

I laughed, and shook my head, then eased her mind by admitting, "I have plenty more. It's the one thing I never seem to run out of."

Tilly linked her arm through mine. I couldn't help get a whiff of aftershave on her cardigan. I must have sniffed loudly as she said, "Do I stink? I did shower, but it was chilly and I nabbed a guy's cardigan."

"It just isn't the smell I'd expected. Nice, but not your perfume."

"Ah, so you noticed my perfume," she teased.

"I did. I have a very strong sense of smell. It's very useful as a chef."

"Of course, you were a top chef, weren't you?" We began to walk while we chatted, and I told her a little about my previous life to pass the time, using it as a useful reminder that I was better off out of that game, and making burritos under a gazebo was my limit nowadays.

"You're a true hobo, like Ben and Russell. It must be such a strange life. No home with lots of rooms. No garden, or a bathroom."

"The whole world is my garden."

"And the whole world is your toilet too. I've seen you guys, always peeing in hedges."

"I try not to, but sometimes I do, yes."

"Get a bottle. You can buy them for a few quid. Special ones for camping."

"I did, actually, and it's been a game-changer. Makes life much easier."

"There you go then!" Tilly hummed happily to

herself as we walked, her fears of earlier seemingly forgotten. What had possessed her to walk alone in the dark all the way to see me I couldn't understand, but she seemed much better for having told me about Tony.

Speaking of which, as we approached the car park where the various buildings were sited, Tilly gasped and pulled up short. I followed her gaze and saw Tony standing outside the pub, leaning against the railing smoking an ecig.

Anxious growled then raced across the empty car park, skidded to a halt next to a startled Tony, and began barking his head off.

"Anxious," I hissed, "stop that! Come here. You'll wake everyone up."

We hurried over and I clipped the littler terror onto his lead, but he wasn't happy about it and continued to growl.

"Hello, Tony," said Tilly nervously, trying to appear brave by stepping away from me.

"Hi. Um, are you the guy who got me into trouble with the law? Max, right?" He looked exhausted, and took a few deep drags on his ecig, lost to clouds of vapour for a moment.

"Sorry about that. I just reported what I'd seen before I found Russell. I saw you and another man close by so told them."

"Fair enough." He shrugged, then continued to smoke. "What's with the dog? Why does he hate me so much?"

"He doesn't hate you, but I think you surprised him."

"Tony, what happened?" asked Tilly. "Who was that man you were with?"

"He's just someone I know. Comes in the pub regularly. We got to chatting then wandered back up here and next thing I knew I was down the station answering questions for hours. They accused me of murder. Murder! Me! I mean, c'mon. You know me. I wouldn't hurt a fly."

"I'm so sorry," squealed Tilly. "I thought it might be you and got myself worked up. I know you would never do it, but I was scared and didn't know what to think."

"Hey, it's okay. I understand. And Max, I don't blame you. I would have done the same thing. It was the right thing to do. Anyway, it's over now, but I'm beat. See you in the morning?" he asked Tilly.

"Absolutely. See you tomorrow."

Tony nodded to us both, then entered the building.

Tilly sighed once the door closed, and moved close to link arms again. "I feel awful for suspecting him now. He really is a good guy. Handsome, too, and always so kind. What is wrong with me?"

"It's a stressful time, and it makes you doubt everything when something like this happens. Don't be too hard on yourself. Get some rest, and things will seem better in the morning."

"Maybe, but two men will still be dead."

"Yes, they will, and nothing we do will ever change that. I'm sorry you lost your friends. I'll see what I can uncover tomorrow."

"Me too. I'll ask around, then let's meet up at some point to share information."

"I don't know when that will be as my folks are here as you know, but we'll definitely do it soon. Sleep well, Tilly."

"Sorry again for disturbing you." Tilly bent, and made a fuss of Anxious whose eyes were still focused on the door. "And you, my new bestie. I apologise for waking you up."

We waited until Tilly was inside, and she locked the door, then headed back to Vee, our steps heavy and slow. The site was deadly quiet now apart from a few stalwarts sitting outside staring at the stars or watching the dying embers of campfires. I couldn't figure out why Tilly had come to see me, despite what she'd said. If she was so scared, why risk the long walk alone? She had nothing to gain by telling me Tony and his buddy were released, and all to lose if she believed they were guilty.

The late hour was definitely getting to me, causing my thoughts to become scrambled and my imagination to run wild. This was what had happened to her, was my guess, and she got herself into a panic. Hopefully, seeing Tony would allow her to calm down and regain her trust in her fellow co-worker.

As long as he was innocent!

We finally made it back to Vee and crawled into bed gratefully, but I couldn't settle even with Anxious breathing heavily beside me and cuddling into him. What confounded me the most about all of this was why the killer had run such a high risk. Carrying a rifle in the middle of the day at a very busy, albeit large, campsite was not what you'd expect from a soldier, especially if they were special ops. They liked to work at night, or in an environment that afforded lots of cover, not wandering around sand dunes and open tracks in full military garb with a massive rifle slung over your shoulder.

After tossing and turning for hours, I finally drifted off, but my sleep was light and unsettled. By six, I couldn't stand it any longer so unlocked the van then quietly exited, leaving the door open so Anxious could join me if he ever woke up.

It was a beautiful morning and already warm, something I would never stop being grateful for, so I stretched out, breathed deeply, and went for a pee before sorting out morning coffee. With a new special blend to try, I focused on that, and once it was brewed I took it with me and had a little stroll, but stayed close so the little guy wouldn't fret if he tried to find me.

Early morning at campsites is even more magical than the night sometimes, probably because there is a huge dose of smugness involved. Knowing you have a good few hours more than everyone else makes you feel truly alive and part of the world, but it's what you get to see that makes it worth doing on occasion. A low mist hung in the higher dunes, making it look like still lakes, and the air had a different quality, especially at the coast. Somehow more salty, more energised by the sea, with a stillness that seeps into your bones and psyche and leaves you truly at peace.

I revelled in the solitude, the lack of thought, the inner calm that radiated out and allowed me to commune with nature and feel part of something bigger yet forever elusive.

Sipping my coffee, I turned my attention to the east and climbed the high dune beside our pitch, the sun slowly revealing itself until I reached the summit and could look out over the huge expanse of terrain. Sunrise had already happened hours ago, but was only just coming over the hills, still low and obscured enough by a thin layer of wispy cloud to allow me to watch it gradually rise and warm the sand and scrub.

This was what life was all about. Connecting, breathing deeply of clean, fresh air, not a soul in sight, just tents and vans and the occasional building, but more gulls than anything as they prepared for a day of hunting and scavenging. I sipped my coffee, utterly content, wondering how my folks had slept and what Min was doing. I hoped she was okay. The last time we were together, mere days ago, she had been upset about life, unsure about the future and concerned about making the wrong decision, and I understood her concerns, but hoped she would choose me to be a part of her plans. It was so difficult for her, as unlike me her life had become more complicated. Min had to pick what kind of life she would like for herself and where to live, how to live, possibly quit her job, leave her home, uproot herself. It was too much. How could she make that decision?

I knew she wanted us to be together again, but also accepted the concerns because they were all down to my past behaviour. She could handle this life, there was no question, but it was still a huge ask when she had no way of knowing what it would be like permanently rather than a few days here and there.

But maybe there was another way, another option, and it had been nagging at me more and more over recent months. I adored vanlife, but I also adored being at campsites and meeting people, offering advice and getting some in return. I had plenty to think about, but now wasn't the time. Now all I had to do was watch the sunrise and drink my amazing coffee.

So that's what I did.

Chapter 11

Once my coffee was drunk and the sun had risen high enough to warm my skin and make it clear the day would be hot bordering on blistering even this early in the season, I took a final deep breath, stretched out my arms, smiled, and turned then slid down the dune back towards our pitch.

As I reached camp, I spied Anxious sitting in the doorway of Vee, yawning then cocking his head, sniffing as his ears twitched, listening for me.

Grinning, as man did I love the little guy, I called out, "Over here."

Anxious' head snapped around, searching the dunes, but he couldn't see me and began to whine as he hopped down and ran around, nose to the ground, following my trail. He went the wrong way.

"No, over here!" I giggled, sliding down the last section of dune.

Anxious raced over, tail wagging like he was trying to snap it off, and I squatted as he launched into my arms, whining with pleasure, and began to lick me.

"Hey, it's alright, good to see you too. Have a nice sleep?"

A happy bark was my answer.

"That's great. I couldn't settle, so got up early and watched the sunrise. It's beautiful. You want to look?"

Anxious stared into my eyes, then squirmed as he blinked rapidly and squinted.

"Oh, yeah, of course. I know that look. Down you get."

Back on terra firma, he trotted off a respectable distance then cocked a leg and let nature become a little more soggy. Deciding I needed at least another coffee if not two to get me going after rising so early, I lit the gas and put the kettle on and sorted out the cafetière, then made breakfast for the always starving pooch.

After a drink of water, Anxious tucked into his food then joined me standing outside the front of the gazebo to watch the world go by, or in our case, absolutely nothing go by as we were tucked away down here, while I sipped my coffee, beyond grateful for such a small but important luxury.

"What do you fancy doing today? I was thinking maybe go up to the farm where Ben worked and see if whoever lives there has any insight into his past. It's worth a shot, and he might have told them more than anyone around here. So far, Ben's a real man of mystery and it's bugging me not knowing who he really was or why anyone might have taken him out like that. What say you, my best buddy?"

A frown, then him wandering off to inspect a thick tuft of grass was all the answer I needed to prove he hadn't understood but was happy to go along with whatever I chose, so to get him in the mood I suggested a walk once we got there.

"Ah, you understand that, don't you?" I snorted, inhaling my coffee the wrong way and ending up in a coughing fit with the bitter liquid dribbling into my beard.

After sorting everything out, and calling my folks to explain, we made the short drive off Shell Island, then headed into the unknown.

I checked the route on my phone as I drove along a narrow road, the farm turn coming up ahead on my left. Glancing at the unruly mess, I hoped this wasn't it, but as I slowed, and the artificial voice told me to take the turn, my spirits darkened—this was the farm alright.

Strewn across multiple fields were endless machines, some intact, plenty little more than rusting heaps of various parts. Large barns hid everything but a glimpse of the farmhouse, towering steel structures cobbled together from various materials and patched over the years, while one stuck out like a sore thumb, pristine and gleaming in the sunshine.

Cows called from fields, sheep grazed, and dogs barked in the distance as we bumped along the pot-holed track. Anxious glanced at me, concerned, so I told him that unfortunately this was the place and to be mindful of any sharp metal.

I parked beside the gate and we got out. Heaped up by the fence posts were old washing machines, several chest freezers, and a rusting engine. I got rather freaked out and imagined the machines coming to life and attacking, a post-apocalyptic rise of the machines scenario where they finally got payback for their mistreatment.

With no bell or any way to announce our arrival, I opened the gate and we headed into the yard. It was filthy with cow muck and the smell was strong, but that wasn't unusual for a farm. What was unusual was the sheer volume of stuff. Obviously, most farms had plenty of machinery, but this was on a scale I'd never encountered before. It was more like a scrap yard than anything, but like none I could have dreamed of. Everywhere I looked were machine parts, stacks of timber, roof sheeting, steel beams, cars piled on top of each other, rusting tractors, some shiny new ones, diggers, tippers, even an old steam roller and a railway carriage.

We kept to the middle away from anything dangerous, and wandered towards the house tucked behind the swanky new barn. Surrounded by a low stone wall at the front, but a high wooden fence around the sides and rear, the cottage had about a third of an acre to itself. The squat stone building had seen better days and needed a new roof and windows, the front door was rotting at the base, and the red paint was peeling so bad I wondered how old it was and if it was dangerous to even breathe near it.

But this wasn't what gave me pause. It was the volume of junk within the walls. If I'd thought the yard and fields were concerning, then this was on a whole other level of hoarding. Stacks of rotting newspapers and magazines, more fridges, old doors, glass, piles of rubble, bricks, stone, earth, random towers of bottles in bags, mounds of blankets, old clothes, mattresses, and pretty much anything that a farm might have once used had seemingly been abandoned outside, leaving nothing but a narrow path to the house.

We eased through the rotten wooden gate and approached gingerly, battling weeds that had given up the fight everywhere but on the path, and were flourishing. The only reason I thought someone actually lived here was because the weeds and grass were flattened along the crumbling red-brick path like someone used it regularly, as otherwise I would have sworn the place was abandoned long ago.

I expected dogs to come tearing over the wall, alerted by our presence, but the barking remained some way off and was probably from another farm. Outside the house, beer bottles, empty cans of food and drink, endless bottles of spirits, and bag upon bag of rubbish were piled up to the windows and beyond. Whoever lived here really was a terrible hoarder. I couldn't imagine what the inside was like, and dreaded knocking, but that's exactly what I did after taking a deep breath. Bad idea, as it stank out here. The problem with rats and mice must be horrendous.

Almost immediately the door was opened, and instead of a foul smell kicking me back and sending me gasping for air, a sweet, almost subtle aroma drifted out on a pleasant, gentle breeze. A quick look past the owner revealed large sliding glass doors that were open onto a beautiful, serene, Japanese-style garden full of small ponds, rocks, manicured lawns, and red acers dancing joyously under the shade of a large variegated sycamore.

The space between me and the rear was littered with more bottles, boxes, books teetering almost to the ceiling, the floor covered in rugs piled haphazardly over one another, making me dizzy with the riot of colour. But it was clean, bordering on immaculate, and left me utterly confounded.

"Hello?" said the woman I had until now hardly glanced at.

"Sorry, I got distracted," I said, focusing on her and smiling.

The owner smiled calmly at me, somehow managing to have both a faraway, serene look in her eyes yet a focused intensity at the same time. She was in her fifties at a guess, with smooth, tanned skin, shoulder length blond hair drifting graciously towards silver, with a subtle hint of make-up around her eyes, and pale pink lips that were full and friendly. She wore a faded pair of blue dungarees cut stylishly short above the ankle, revealing dainty, bare feet with red-painted nails. I knew I was lingering looking at them, so snapped my head up to be greeted by her amused smile.

"Like feet, do you?" she laughed.

"Not especially, although yours are very nice. Sorry, where are my manners? I'm Max. I apologise for calling on you unannounced, but I was told that Ben worked here. Have you heard the news?"

Her smile faded, replaced with a downturn of the lips and a genuine sadness as she nodded mutely. I let her regain her composure, then she said, "Terrible what happened. We thought so highly of Ben. He was like family. Like a brother to us both."

"Us?"

"Me and my husband. He's around somewhere. Probably tinkering with an engine. He's never happier than when he's covered in oil and making a mess. I'm Willow. Nice to meet you, Max." Willow glanced at the chaos surrounding us, then explained, "I gave up trying to get rid of this junk years ago. I just can't do it. It started out with a few newspapers I wanted to keep, then my husband got into his machinery and it snowballed. I'm afraid we both have a frightful issue with hoarding and can't seem to break free of it. Oh well!" She laughed and smiled, seemingly at peace with her nature.

"Is it okay if we have a chat about Ben? I know this is out of the blue, but I'm staying at Shell Island and was the last person to see him alive. I'm the one who found him too. I also found his friend, Russell, and, er, the killer kidnapped my dog and locked him in a cupboard in Ben's van.

"Oh, you poor thing!" Willow bent, and Anxious, not missing a trick, held up his paw and cocked his head. "Is he hurt?" she asked me.

"No, just trying to play the sympathy card and get a treat."

"Then let's go inside and see what we can find. We don't have a dog at the moment. We lost our little darling a few months back, but I'm sure there are plenty of biscuits in the cupboard. He was a Labrador, and you know what they're like about food."

Anxious didn't need telling twice and raced inside, barking for us to get a move on.

"Sorry about him. He hears the word biscuit and forgets his manners."

"Oh, that's not a problem." Willow laughed, her nature seemingly always happy. "We have people and animals in and out all the time. Sometimes you can't move in the kitchen for lambs or piglets. It's the way it is on farms."

"That must be fun." I couldn't imagine the chaos, but I could picture Min happily feeding lambs from a bottle in a farmhouse kitchen and loving every minute of it.

"Come in, come in. No need to worry about the dog. What's his name?"

"Anxious. Not by nature though," I added hurriedly, hoping to forego the usual explanation about it not being his emotional state.

"Ha! How lovely. We had a dog called Happy once, as he was the cutest thing you ever saw when a puppy and seemed to always be smiling."

"Oh, did he turn out to be rather serious?"

Willow turned back from the hallway and frowned. "No, he was happy his entire life. Always so much fun."

"Er, okay."

"Take your boots off, please. It might be chaos, but it's clean chaos."

"Of course." I removed my boots, pleased I'd worn them rather than Crocs because of the yard, then entered what could best be described as an Aladdin's cave of mostly worthless treasure.

I followed Willow along the surprisingly generous hallways, the dark flagstones buried beneath the rugs and piles of stuff, and entered the expansive kitchen. Work had clearly been done at some point, doubling the footprint of the building, as the kitchen was enormous.

"Wow, this is impressive. So big."

"I do love a huge kitchen. I'm a keen cook."

"Me too, but I live in a VW so usually cook outside. I'm jealous."

"Aw, that's so sweet, but I know what you're really thinking. How can anyone cook in a place so rammed with stuff? There's not a bare work surface to be seen. Everything's covered in books or crockery or lamps or bits of engines, and I can tell you're a very neat and tidy man. Bit OCD, I'm guessing."

"I am, and yes, it isn't exactly how I'd have my kitchen, but it seems to suit you and your lifestyle and personality."

"You're being very diplomatic," chuckled Willow, a real twinkle in her eye. She seemed to find everything amusing, and wasn't concerned with what anyone thought about her, which I found refreshing but disturbing as how could she not see this was no way to live? I was being judgemental, I knew, but could never understand this type of behaviour as much as I tried to. It just didn't fit with my worldview, and I knew that wasn't fair. My obsessive nature and attention to the minutest of details was seen as completely over-the-top by many, yet I accepted it as part of who I was.

"You must have been here a long time to have accumulated so many things." I tried to take in the extent of the hoarding, but it was hard as there was simply so much stuff. One entire wall was taken up by a massive coat rack with at least fifty coats of all description, with nigh on a hundred pairs of shoes, boots, wellies, sandals, trainers, and assorted umbrellas and walking sticks.

The counters were overflowing with kitchen equipment, stacks of papers, and broken machines. The floor was piled high with boxes, various small engines in different stages of being either dismantled or rebuilt, their innards like a postmortem on a mechanical corpse, and the eight-seater classic scrubbed pine table had no space to sit and eat at, with over thirty oil lamps, ornaments, and more books and papers.

"We moved in the day we got married decades ago. It's the family farm on my husband's side and we inherited along with the land when his parents retired. I'd never leave. Now, where did I put those biscuits?"

Anxious looked up from sniffing the footwear, his hackles up, but the love of biscuits was too strong so he hurried over, claws clattering on the stone floor, and skidded to a halt beside Willow as she bent and rummaged in an overflowing cupboard. She stood holding a box of biscuits like a prize. "Ah, here we are. Anxious, will you sit like a good boy?"

Anxious barked and dutifully sat, tail thudding against the floor, not a speck of dust circulating. How on earth did she clean?

"He's never better behaved than when a treat's about to arrive," I giggled.

"Then you deserve it." Willow held out a bone-shaped biscuit and Anxious took it politely then lay down and devoured it before she even had the chance to get a second one from the box. He sat up, ears primed, drooling. He was given another, then Willow told him that would be all, so he took his time; it was still gone by the time she put the box away.

"Let's go out the back into the garden. It's my favourite place in the whole world. Would you like a cup of tea?"

"Tea would be great. Are you sure I'm not inconveniencing you?"

"Of course not! It's lovely to have visitors, and if this helps get justice for Ben, then of course I can find the time."

"Thank you. That's very kind."

We chatted while the tea was made, then I followed Willow through the sliding doors and into what felt like another world. It took my breath away as from the inside you couldn't appreciate how magical the back garden was. To call it a garden didn't do it justice though. It was more like a Zen garden, or a park or something I had no words to describe—it was so at odds with the rest of the property it made my head spin.

The heavenly perfume made me sneeze, and as I patted my pocket for a tissue, Willow handed me a handkerchief. "It's freshly laundered. Keep it. It will bring you luck."

"Thanks. But how will it bring me luck?"

"Because you will be able to blow your nose properly," she teased, smiling.

"How is this garden here? I mean, it's so different from everything else."

"My oasis." Willow's love for her garden was obvious. She seemed to fill up with the joy it gave her and it spilled over, radiating out into every corner, enveloping me.

Anxious cocked his head and looked at me, so I asked Willow if he could explore and she told him that would be fine but not to mess up anything or pee on the rocks. He trotted off, carefully following the meandering paths, leaving the moss-covered rocks alone.

"It's remarkable. It must have taken so much work."

"It's been years, but more than worth it. I know my nature, and my husband's, but there's always another side to people, isn't there?" She cocked her head, studying me intensely, reminding me of Anxious.

"Always. Everyone has two sides to them."

"So, here we have it! My contradictory nature in evidence. It's the only place where I refuse to have a single thing that doesn't fit. I cleared the whole garden myself many years ago, then set to work. I planted the acers, the hostas, fuchsia, and ferns, sowed the grass seed, got my husband and Ben to shift the rocks, placed them exactly where they were meant to be, and slowly it took shape. Now I simply adore it and spend more time here than anywhere else. Ben was a great help, too, of course. He put in an inordinate amount of work to get it to what you see today."

"So he's been working here for a long time?"

"Years and years. An odd fellow, but a real sweetheart too. We got on very well. Most likely because he was like me. A hoarder. But he also enjoyed the simplicity of his life. Mine may be rather more chaotic than his had been for decades, but we were on the same page. He had his van, his outdoorsy life with his tents and whatnot, and I have this."

We took a seat at a simple wooden bench beside a small pond where goldfish darted to and fro in the dark pool, hiding under miniature lily pads or sunning themselves in the shallows where pebbles stored the heat of the day.

"It's okay to talk about Ben? As I told you, I spoke to him before he died, then found him. And his friend the next day. Russell. Did you know him?"

"A little, but not as well as Ben. Russell worked here sometimes, but mostly it was Ben. Ben was like family. He stayed at the farm for months sometimes, either in that grotty van of his or one of the barns. We always told him he could stay in the house, but that wasn't the kind of life he wanted for himself. I understood. He had a terrible past, and this was just how he had decided to live. A loner, but oh boy could he talk once he got going." Willow chuckled as she brushed a strand of hair from her cheek as a gentle breeze blew past, disturbing the acers, the red leaves glistening. A soft, hypnotic scent teased me with a promise of flowers hidden around a bend in the garden.

"Can I be frank?"

"Only if I can be Jasmine. I've always liked the name." Willow laughed at her own joke, utterly calm and at ease.

I laughed politely and asked, "Why do you think he was murdered?"

"I presume it's to do with his past. Ben never discussed it in detail, but from what I've gathered over the years, he was some kind of super secret soldier involved in very dangerous missions. Real top secret stuff. He would never be drawn on the subject, but he said enough. He had to leave, but couldn't settle, and had to get away from anything that reminded him of his past, so ended up in the area with his van. He bummed around, did odd jobs, and over the years became a bit of a local character. An absolutely incorrigible liar, which both amused and annoyed the hell out of me, I nevertheless grew to think very highly of him."

"And he worked hard? Was never any trouble? Did anyone ever come looking for him?"

"He was a very hard worker, and no, there was never any trouble or anyone knocking at my door asking about him apart from you and the police and a rather peculiar detective. I told them what I'm telling you. He was a fine fellow but lied like his life depended on it. Just his way. I think it was a defence mechanism to cope with the past. A way to distance himself."

Anxious returned looking happy, then his ears pricked up and he barked. A man appeared in the doorway to the kitchen and Willow said, "Ah, here's Owen now." She patted Anxious, who took her relaxed cue and lay down, but he kept his eyes locked on Owen.

"Your son?" I asked, noting the man of about my age tugging at a tweed coat and removing a flat cap.

Willow raised an eyebrow? "Son? I have no son. That's Owen, my husband."

"Oh, I'm so sorry. I didn't mean to say that—"

Willow held up a hand and smiled. "Max, relax, it's fine. We're twenty years apart in age, and he's probably as young as you, but make no mistake, his mind is that of a sixty-year-old farmer." Willow giggled, then rose to go and speak to her husband who hadn't spotted us yet.

Chapter 12

From what I heard, Willow was simply explaining who I was, and her husband, Owen, sounded fine about it. They had a quick chat about what he'd been doing, something to do with sheep, then she asked if he wanted a cuppa. He did. Willow called to ask if I wanted another. I refused, then stood to greet Owen as he approached.

He wasn't your typical squat, well-built farmer type, but was slim and strong like his wife, with a ruddy complexion, thick eyebrows over dark eyes, a buzzcut, and wore jeans and a check shirt with the sleeves rolled up revealing powerful forearms and fingers thick from manual labour. He had an open, jovial face, but the overriding feeling I got was simply that he was so young. He made me feel old, even though we were about the same age. Maybe it was the farm and the junk, or the way he moved. Willow was right; he seemed like an ageing farmer, not a young man. How could someone my age have had the opportunity to amass so much stuff?

"Hey, Max, is it?" Owen extended a hand and we shook.

"Yes, and you're Owen?"

"I am. Nice to meet you. And who's this?" Owen bent and rubbed Anxious' head then straightened out, his back clicking.

Anxious backed away and lowered his head, then tentatively stepped forward and sniffed Owen's legs before retreating and siting beside me. Sometimes he didn't take to people, and Owen clearly wasn't that interested either and was merely being polite.

"Tiring morning?"

"Very. Sheep wrangling for the most part."

"Sounds like hard work. Oh, this is Anxious."

"Aw, what's the matter, little fella?"

Anxious sat and lifted a paw, but for once it failed to impress and Owen bent to him again, wagged a finger, and reprimanded him. "You shouldn't pretend to be poorly. Otherwise, when you are, nobody will believe you. But I get that it was worth a shot." He chuckled as he stood, his back clicking again, leaving Anxious' jaw slack.

"Ha! In your face, Anxious! See, I told you not to keep doing that."

Disgruntled, he slunk off to see if he could "help" in the kitchen.

"Take a seat, Max."

We sat on the bench and Owen sighed as he cast his eyes around the garden.

"It's a beautiful place," I noted.

"Stunning. We need it. This has been a lifesaver. You've seen the rest of the farm, so know we have issues. I grew up like this, stuff everywhere, and when I inherited fifteen years ago I just carried right on where my folks left off. The lucky things now live in a bungalow with a neat garden and left their hoarder ways behind, but I can't shake it. Terrible affliction."

"Everyone has a burden to carry. Did Willow explain why I'm here?"

"She did. You're looking into Ben and Russell's death. Bad business that. Has military written all over it. Ben was a good bloke. We liked him. He obviously had a dark past, but we enjoyed his company and he was a hard worker."

"I guess he's worked here since before you inherited."

"A few years, yes. But it was only once we took over that he became more of a fixture. He'd spend a few months here, then go off who knew where, then come back for a while and in the better weather he'd usually be at the campsite or travelling around the area. He never seemed to stray far, but didn't ever tell us where he'd been either."

"What do you think happened?"

Owen shrugged. "My best guess is that it's something to do with his army days. He got shot in the head, right?" I nodded. Owen grunted. "Sounds like a pro. He never told us about his past, and we stopped asking, but it has to be that. Russell was army, too, and was more open about it. A regular soldier, but Ben was different. He was haunted. You could see it in his eyes. He had issues, that was for sure, but he did his work, was no bother, and I liked the guy."

"Is there anything you can tell me that might help me uncover who did it? Anything at all? Something he let slip? Anybody he talked about, or something else?"

"Max, I wish there was, but there's nothing. He was a loner, a real dark horse, and he kept himself to himself a lot. Sure, he was a real chatterbox at times, especially after he'd had a few drinks, but it was mostly nonsense. I've never met anyone who lied like he did. It was as though he couldn't help himself. He even seemed to believe half the tales he told. It was messed up, he was messed up, but we did what we could to look after him. I was only young when we married, but he was always around, and we got on well. He didn't mind that I was still just a kid really, and neither did Willow." Owen laughed, like he'd been through a lot of grief because of the age difference, and clearly felt like he had to explain. "We're twenty years apart in age, but our minds are in sync and we love each other. I knew the moment I set eyes on her that Willow was the gal for me, and she felt the same way."

"Then that sounds perfect. I don't judge, and being happy is all we can ask for."

"Too true." Owen slapped me on the back and

laughed, then winced as his back clicked. "I'm getting too old for this life already, but I'll never give it up. It's in the blood and in my heart, you know?"

"I do. It's a passion. A way of life."

Owen shifted, clearly having something to say, then came out with it. "Max, it's a bit weird you being here. What's your interest? Why are you so involved? I know you found them, but the cops are dealing with it, so why are you asking us questions?"

"I feel like I owe it to them. Well, to Ben mostly. It's like a calling, I suppose. Over the last year, I've been around quite a few crazy situations and try to help if I can."

"Fair enough, I suppose. Sorry, mate, but there's not much to tell. We don't know any of his friends from back in the army days. He never told us where he came from originally, and it wasn't for a lack of trying. Ben was a man with no past we know of, just a loner who wanted to enjoy the outdoors, do as he pleased, and have a hot meal. A simple guy, but about as complicated a person as you're ever likely to meet. If you can figure this out, everyone would be grateful. He was well-liked and one of those people you wanted to look out for, you know what I mean?"

"I do. I'll try my best. Thank you for talking to me, and thank you for letting me see this amazing garden."

"Hey, you have Ben and Willow to thank for that, right, love?" Owen stood as Willow approached with his tea.

"Ben worked hard here. Really hard."

"It's just a shame about the tree." Owen pointed to the only mar on the otherwise pristine landscape. The thick trunk of an acer poked out of the ground, having clearly been cut down, leaving the area looking out of balance with everything else.

"It really is. It was my pride and joy. Ben and I planted it almost fifteen years ago. But it got damaged and had to be cut down. I'm hoping it will sprout again, and there do seem to be little buds forming on the trunk." Willow looked ready to burst into tears, and Owen put his arm around her shoulders. "I'm sorry, I know it's just a tree, but it was so special, and I spent so many hours tending to it, feeding it, pruning it, and now it's gone."

"It was a special tree," agreed Owen. "Cost a fortune too," he teased, trying to lighten the mood.

"I'll leave you to it. I can see myself out. Thank you again for your time. Come on, Anxious."

"Oh, wait, Max!" called Willow. "Look at the collared doves at the end of the garden. Aren't they so pretty?"

I turned and noticed Owen put on a pair of glasses then look at the doves, and I returned to them and we watched for a while.

"They make the best sound when they fly," I noted, smiling. As if to prove it, they took to the wing and we all laughed.

We shook hands, then left, battling through the chaos outside the house, then the yard, until we were back in the van and could relax.

Sitting in our seats, Anxious and I stared at each other, at a loss for words, then I asked, him, "What on earth was that all about?"

He whined, lay down, and covered his eyes with his paws.

"Yes, I agree. Imagine if we lived like that. We'd go crazy in a week." I wasn't exaggerating either. I knew I was rather obsessive, but not in a way that was too extreme. I simply liked to have things in their place and to be able to find the things I used without tearing my home apart. Being surrounded by useless stuff was my idea of hell, and although I understood how it could happen to people, the incongruous rear garden that Willow and Owen clearly adored seemed to make it appear more bizarre as they obviously enjoyed clutter-free, serene spaces so much.

I turned Vee around and we headed back to the campsite. It had been worth making the visit, but I was disappointed they couldn't shed any light on Ben's past and he remained a man of mystery. Maybe talking to his old friends more would give me additional information, but I got the feeling they'd said all they were going to say about their time together and were as in the dark as everyone else as to why someone would murder two men at a campsite in such an extreme manner.

At the site, I decided to pop in to reception. Tilly was focused on the computer screen when I entered, but looked up and smiled, eyes full of anticipation as though she expected me to have news. I shook my head and her smile faltered, but then she brightened and said, "At least you've been trying. No news at all?"

"I went up to the farm, but it was a wasted trip. What a crazy place. Listen, can we talk later? I promised the little guy a walk, but we didn't get around to it. That okay?"

"Sure, Max. Thank you for trying. We'll chat later."

Chapter 13

An insistent bark the minute we returned to our pitch meant I now had no choice but to take Anxious right away. I grabbed the lead and my satchel containing poo bags, a bottle of water, and one of many collapsible bowls that seemed to multiply like rabbits in a field of carrots and no farmer for miles. After Vee was locked, I said goodbye to her, which caused me to pause and wonder when I'd started doing that, then we headed off, two guys with a spring in their step and a whole glorious day ahead of them.

If I'd thought watching the sunrise over the dunes at just gone six was magical, being on the beach was like stepping into a true wonderland. Every single time I managed to get down to the shore by midmorning, or earlier if possible, was like a revelation, but I always somehow seemed to forget how spectacular and awe-inspiring it was.

Anxious was his usual energetic self, dashing this way and that, chasing seagulls who taunted him by swooping low, sometimes landing and waiting for him to catch up, only to flap back up into the sky and screech at him as he pelted across the damp sand, tongue out, eyes keen and nothing on his mind but the thrill of the chase.

The wind ruffled my long hair, thick with salt and in need of a wash, but who cared? I didn't. My beard was becoming rather hard to get my fingers through, but I knew a good comb and some beard oil would sort it out, and I'd try to catch a shower later on. I peeled off my vest and revelled in the feel of the sun on my bare skin, relaxing my muscles just for the sensation.

Next, the Crocs came off, and I banged them together to remove the sand then stowed them in my satchel to leave my hands free. The sand was cold and squishy beneath my feet, and my toes sank into spots, making me laugh. I took a leisurely pace and followed Anxious down to the water's edge, then splashed in the shallows even though it was absolutely freezing.

For a while, I stared out to sea, marvelling at the horizon, wondering if I could really see the curvature of the earth or it looked flat. A boat appeared then vanished, bobbing on the swell, but then my attention was caught by something breaking the water close to shore. I was transfixed as I watched a pod of porpoise surface then arc gracefully back under before repeating it time after time.

"You don't get this in the burbs," I sighed, knowing I was feeling smug, but not caring. Part of me wished that every day could be like this, that there was no winter to struggle through, no short days and oh-so-long nights where it was dark by half four and the evenings seemed to stretch out to intolerable lengths. But then such days wouldn't feel so magical, and there'd be no flow of the seasons. Still, sun every day and no winter clothes to store sounded nice too!

After the porpoise moved down the coast, we had a proper walk, going as far as we could one way before turning around and marching back until I began to tire. Anxious would have happily continued all day, but would be utterly exhausted and grumpy if I let that happen, so we took a breather for water, sat on the sand for a while to catch our breath and watch the birds, then headed back towards our starting point.

A woman riding a horse bareback smiled and said hello as she passed, the horse stopping to sniff Anxious. The filly's snort made him jump then run around the mighty beast as I laughed and the woman giggled. We watched them ease into a gentle canter, then its muscles seemed to suddenly fire, and in seconds the horse was racing across the sand and then the shallow water as the tide receded. How wonderful.

We greeted people out for a morning stroll, smiling faces and a few words lifting our spirits, and several dog walkers had a chat with me while Anxious and his new temporary best buddy ran around playing games only they understood, before Anxious came back to my side and we continued on our way until the next encounter. This was one of the wonders of living with a dog. It opened up a whole new world of conversation and smiles from strangers you might never otherwise get a chance to talk to. The animals brought you together, and always elicited a smile no matter your mood otherwise.

Now thoroughly tired out, we returned to where we'd started then began to retrace our steps back up the beach. When we hit the dry sand where the tide hadn't reached, we paused and turned to look back at the water sparkling as the sun grew higher and the sand finally became warm underfoot.

Lost to the majesty of this little slice of Welsh paradise, I snapped out of it as Anxious barked wildly. I turned to face whatever he was unhappy about and spied a battered green Land Rover Defender come peeling towards us, kicking up sand in its wake like it carried a storm under the chassis and was trying to escape it.

Anxious was going nuts by now as the filthy vehicle bounced over the rough terrain and landed with a thud before the driver gunned the engine, dropped a gear and sped up, heading straight for us. I bent and snatched up Anxious, unsure which way to run or if this was just joy-riders out for a morning jolly, but something told me I should run, and run fast.

My best bet was the water, so I peeled down the beach, the going firm at first but becoming increasingly difficult as the sand became soft underfoot. I glanced behind and noted the jeep was gaining on us and was going to cut us off at an angle. I changed tack and ran parallel to the shore for a while, not wanting to risk having to slow down by getting too close to the water, but wondering if the Defender could cope if I did.

Anxious whined, so I soothed him as best I could between my laboured breathing, then switched him to under one arm so I could use the other to pump and get some speed up. A quick check and I knew there was no way I could make it to the water without them catching us, so I zig-zagged back up the beach onto dry sand, heading for a high dune I knew the vehicle couldn't climb.

With salt stinging my eyes, sweat building, Anxious howling, and my speed slowing as the dry sand made the going so difficult, the dune was looming now and I was going to make it. With a final burst of speed, I pumped my legs for all they were worth, the muscles screaming as lactic acid built.

I stumbled, and a twinge in my knee made me gasp, but I righted myself before I fell and thanked my lucky stars I hadn't injured myself, staggering forward towards the base of the dunes.

The Defender skidded to a halt right in front of us, the cloud of sand so dense I couldn't see. I rubbed at my eyes, the grit scratchy, but I had to get away. In a blind panic, I ran left, but as the dust cloud cleared I realised my mistake as I was running straight into the 4x4 that had reversed to cut me off.

The front door snapped out sideways, the boot banged open, and three men in camouflage wearing balaclavas jumped out, their military boots gleaming in the harsh light reflected off the sand. They checked the area and spread out, then charged.

Anxious barked a warning, but they paid him no heed, and before I had the chance to react I was pinned from behind and the other two lunged. One grabbed my waist while the other dove for my feet, tripped me back, and I was caught by the man behind while the others lifted me off the ground. In a flash, I was being bundled into the dirty rear of the Defender. It smelled of oil and earth, but was empty apart from a few duffle bags. I kicked and screamed, clutching Anxious tight, but it was no use as all three were on me now, tying my arms after they tore Anxious from my grasp. He snarled and attacked, but got nothing but a mouthful of thick coat for his troubles before he was shut into a small crate hidden under a blanket that was then covered over again, plunging the poor guy into darkness. He whimpered and whined and it broke my heart.

The men exchanged a glance as if concerned, but then my world turned black, too, as a balaclava was slipped over my head then spun around so I couldn't see and I was pressed down onto the bench seat. My arms were raised above my head and I was clearly being tied to the framework. There they hung, useless and already aching, as I kicked out manically before my legs were secured in a similar fashion. I was utterly defenceless.

It must have all taken less than thirty seconds, then the rear door slammed shut and I heard the driver settle in the front. The engine roared and we skidded before he got traction, then we zoomed across the sand for several minutes in complete silence before we hit the road and everything settled down.

How were they going to get out without being seen? Surely the bloke manning the exit barrier would have something to say about these guys and the wailing dog? Maybe they hadn't thought this through. I got the sinking suspicion that they had, though, and soon enough my suspicions were confirmed.

We stopped and the men moved around in the Land Rover. Something was tied tight over my mouth and then what I assumed was a blanket was draped over my head and body. I could feel the itchy material on my hands.

My gag was removed and I was warned, "Make sure the dog stays quiet or it won't end well," by a man's voice, not a young fella either.

"Anxious, you must be quiet. Only for a little while, okay?"

He whined pitifully; I don't think I'd felt more angry in my life.

"It's okay, nothing bad will happen. Be a good boy."

With a grunt from my captor, the gag was put back in place, the truck started, and we drove on.

When we stopped again, I could make out low voices from outside. The driver said something and I heard the creak of the barrier being raised then we were through and speeding up.

Anxious began to whimper and scratch at the cage, then barked loudly, the sound deafening in the confined space.

My gag was removed, so I explained, "These men won't hurt us. It's just a game. Stay calm and it will be over soon."

Anxious whined again then stayed quiet.

"Well done," said the same voice as earlier. "Just chill, and this will work out fine."

"If you're going to kill me, please don't hurt my dog. He hasn't done anything wrong. If you think I deserve it for trying to find out who killed Ben and Russell, then so be it, but he's a good boy and doesn't deserve this. He can live with my ex-wife. She'll take care of him and he won't bite you unless you let him out, so please drop him off somewhere with a note and her phone number. Please?"

There was an awkward silence, then a different voice said, "See, I told you this was a terrible idea. We should have used my plan and just gone and talked to this guy, not kidnapped him and that cute dog."

"Maybe you're right," conceded the other passenger, "but it's done now. We needed to be sure he was on our side, and now it seems he is. What do you reckon, Phil, let him loose?"

"May as well. If Max thought he was going to be killed and still admitted to trying to help, and was more worried about his dog than himself, then he's a good guy in my book. We'll be there in a minute, so wait until then, but,

Max, we're so sorry about this."

"Um, okay," I said warily, having absolutely no idea what on earth was going on here, but obviously beyond relieved I wasn't about to be shot in the head and thrown out of the back door into a ditch before they killed Anxious too.

Not wanting to rock the boat, as I still had no clue what was happening or why, I said nothing to the men who also didn't speak but focused on keeping Anxious calm as he was beginning to freak out. He whined, and scratched at the cage, but the more I soothed him the more he began to relax, and soon he settled.

No sooner had he calmed than we pulled up somewhere, the sound of gravel making me assume we were at a house. My bonds were untied, but the balaclava remained on. The doors were opened, then I was guided outside. I was held by the arm as someone clattered around in the back—from what I heard tell, they were dragging the crate closer to the door.

My balaclava was pulled over my head and I parted my hair so I could see, to find that I was staring at Anxious in his crate, his eyes two massive brown saucers of concern and fear.

I reached out to unlock him, then turned to check I wasn't about to get clobbered for doing something I wasn't meant to, to find the three men sitting on rocks and staring at me.

"Can I let him out?"

"Of course. Don't hate us too much. We didn't know what else to do. Please, go ahead. Don't order him to attack. That won't end well for any of us."

I nodded, then turned back to the little guy and undid the latch then caught him when he jumped into my arms. He licked my face in a panic, tail thumping slowly against my chest, whining all the while.

"It's alright. We're safe now." I stroked his back, rubbed his head, and scratched behind his ears while he mewled and glanced repeatedly over my shoulder at our attackers "You're okay. We're safe," I repeated.

"I wouldn't say you're safe, mate," growled one of them.

I turned to find them standing right behind me, their balaclavas removed, looking grim and ready to attack.

Chapter 14

"Hey, hold on a minute! You said we were safe. Now you're going to kill us?" I stepped back until I was hard against the vehicle, Anxious held tight in my arms, his fur on end and his teeth bared as he growled menacingly.

"Whoa! You got it all wrong. We won't hurt you. I meant that the killer's still on the loose so you aren't safe. We're here to help. To get justice for Ben and this Russell guy, whoever he is. We haven't got all the intel yet, but seems like he was ex-military, too, and a buddy of Ben's. Any friend of his is a friend of ours. We owe him our lives."

The others murmured their agreement and visibly relaxed.

"I don't understand any of this. What the hell is going on? What do you think you're doing? You storm the campsite, kidnap us, and now you expect me to believe you won't hurt us? What gives?"

"Max, take a seat and let us explain," said the man who had yet to say more than a few words.

"Where is this place?"

"Old quarry. Deserted now. Close to Shell Island, but there's nothing and nobody here. We won't be disturbed."

"Who are you guys?"

All three wore their camouflage gear, but stripped back to combat trousers, boots, and vests. Not one of them was under sixty, with dark tans, plenty of lines, and one had short-cropped grey hair while the other two had long hair tied back in ponytails. Their bare arms were covered in faded tattoos and scars, each frame wiry and clearly powerful despite their age.

The man with the short hair and green vest stepped forward and said, "I'm Phil." He hitched a thumb to the man on his left. "This is Gummo, and the other misfit is Shorty. Before you ask, yes, they have nicknames from way back, but I don't. Just the way it was and it stuck."

"You're all ex-military? Army?"

"How did you guess?" laughed Gummo, his prominent gums and incredibly white full set of teeth clearly the reason for the nickname.

"We served for a long time, but we've been out for nearly as long as we were in," said Shorty, dragging on his ponytail and frowning, his six foot three powerful frame the obvious reason for his nickname. "Some of us from the gang kept in touch, others we lost contact with and never heard from again. Some are dead, others wanted to put the past behind them, but Ben was one of us and when we heard what happened, we came as soon as we could. Now we want answers."

"You served together with Ben?"

"Sure did," said Phil, who seemed to be if not in charge then the one they let take the lead. "He's our mate, always will be. We lost touch a long time ago. Ben went off the rails, but we sorted him out for a while. Then he left and we never heard from him again. Now we've found him, but it's too late. We were forwarded a picture from a friend and it sounded and looked like Ben, so we came to check it out. We asked around, and it was definitely him. No mistake. Mates for life. Brothers. That's what we are. He's one of us."

"And what exactly is that? What did you do in the army?"

"Enough questions for now. Let's have a brew and get to know each other a little first. We know some of what happened, but not all, and it seems like you're the man in the know. Sorry about all this, but we had to be sure. For all we knew, it was you and you were covering your tracks, but you pan out, and we just needed to have a word in private. We were in two minds about you, Max, but now we're convinced you're a decent bloke. The way you handled yourself in the old Defender, and how you wanted to keep your dog safe, tells us what we need to know about your character. So relax, okay?"

"I'll try."

"Good man." Phil beamed at me, then stepped forward and slapped me on the back with a chuckle. "I gotta hand it to you, I'm impressed. You were one cool cookie. You'd have made an excellent soldier, or possibly a spy."

"So I've been told. I had an offer not so long ago. The spook business isn't for me though."

"Don't blame you!" he laughed. "Take a seat, Max. You too, Anxious." Phil smiled at us, then bent to Anxious who backed off a little and looked to me for advice.

"You don't have to be friends, but no biting," I explained.

Anxious sat, and was very brave as Phil reached out a hand, but he refused to let the man touch him.

Phil shrugged and said, "Fair enough. I guess I deserve much worse. Listen up, Anxious. We won't hurt you or Max, but you both need to stay with us for a while to let us explain things. That okay? There's a biscuit in it for you."

Anxious' ears perked up, but when Phil pulled a biscuit out of his pocket and offered it to my brave little guy Anxious did the impossible and turned his head away.

"I guess I deserve that," sighed Phil, looking genuinely remorseful. He dropped the biscuit, stood, and said, "We'll make a brew. You guys get comfortable over there on that large slab of granite. It's warm and safe, so just relax for a few." Phil nodded to his friends and they moved to the rear of the Defender. The moment they were away from us Anxious snaffled the biscuit, grinned cheekily at me, then followed me over to the huge slab of rock.

I sat and he hopped up then settled on my lap, the closeness welcome for us both. The quarry had clearly been deserted decades ago with algae and plants in dark, damp crevices, small patches of water in hollows, and ivy sprawling everywhere, even hanging from above like living ropes. High cliffs surrounded us, with ancient tracks now treacherous where landslides had made them impassable. It was a beautiful spot, and perfect for committing murder and getting away with it. I shuddered despite the heat radiating from the granite, and turned my focus to the men.

They had pulled out a small table from the Land Rover and were boiling a battered kettle on a single ring gas stove like the one I had. Shorty was spooning coffee into tin mugs while Gummo was splashing milk into them. The men spoke in whispers interspersed with an occasional laugh or a turn of the head to presumably check we hadn't run off.

What would be the point? I had no idea where to go, and they could obviously catch us if we tried. If it was life or death, then of course I would attempt to escape, but it really did seem like they were on the level. They sure had a funny way of operating though. I mean, who did this kind of thing? It was nuts.

Anxious shot upright as the men returned, a menacing growl emanating from deep inside his chest. I stroked his head and reassured him that everything was fine, but he was understandably reticent to make friends after the ordeal they'd put him through.

"We really are so sorry about doing this to you both. I know it must have been very scary," said Phil. "Anxious, please forgive us. We love dogs, and would never harm one, but we didn't want to leave you behind. The cage was for your own protection, and ours, as the last thing we wanted was a fight with someone as strong and ferocious as you."

The little guy puffed out his chest and nodded, so I patted his back and confirmed how brave and intimidating he was.

Gummo handed me a steaming mug and said, "Phil's right. It's been a bit of a mad rush and we cobbled together this plan without much time to consider the finer details. Right nightmare it's been."

"Not as much as for Ben and that other bloke," said Shorty.

"Why storm in like that and kidnap us? Thanks for the coffee." I sipped, my eyes widening. "Wow, that's good. I thought it was instant."

"It is, but my own special blend," said Shorty proudly.

"Look, guys, I'm sure you mean well, but you can't go around kidnapping people and animals and expect them to be happy about it. If you're old friends of Ben's, why not ask for a chat with me? And why me anyway? I only met the guy once for a few minutes, so I'm hardly an authority on him."

"That's not the point. Once we heard about him going missing, we got together and decided we'd come and help search. We haven't seen him in decades. Then when it was reported he was dead, we looked into everyone involved and your name stood out for obvious reasons. Max Effort, professional vanlifer, ex-chef, amateur detective with an incredible knack for solving the seemingly unsolvable. We had to get you alone, and we had to talk to you properly without the chance of anyone stopping us."

"Plus, we worried you might get killed for interfering," added Gummo with a wide grin that almost blinded me.

"So you think the killer hasn't finished yet?" I asked, raising an eyebrow, the steam from the mug beading on my forehead.

The men exchanged a look, then Phil shrugged and admitted, "Mate, we have no bleedin' idea what's going on. All we know is that Ben was one of us and we never leave a man behind. Understand?"

"Kind of. Why did you lose touch?"

"We were tight, I mean really tight, but one by one we left the forces. Some of us returned to our home towns, some of us moved away, but all of us were messed up, broken if you like. Adjusting to civilian life is unbelievably difficult after spending all of your adult life living by army rules. You don't have a clue how it really works out in the world. Sure, we had leave, but we were single blokes and when we got time off, we'd travel and mostly mess around."

"He means we'd blow all our cash going to crazy places and getting drunk and chasing women," said Gummo with a smirk.

"Yeah, maybe." Phil shook his head at Gummo, telling him that wasn't helping. "Anyway, we were tight, but wild, and unprepared for houses or flats, mortgages, bills, dealing with regular people. It was so predictable, so boring, so mundane. Some of us moved into private security, several went absolutely bananas, and some like Ben just vanished. He hung around for a while, tried to make a go of things, but then he was gone. Just gone. We didn't hear a word from him after. This was way back, decades ago, and one by one everyone either settled into regular life and didn't want to be involved with the others, or died, and then it was just us three. Been like it for many years now. We stay in touch with a few blokes, but the real gang was us and Ben. We missed him, tried everything to find him, but never even got a sniff. Until now."

"How did you hear about him disappearing then dying?" I asked, curious despite wanting to get out of here.

"We know people. We've had feelers out for several of the troop for a very long time." Phil glanced at the others again and they both nodded. Clearly, they hadn't discussed exactly how much they were willing to share with me.

"And they got in touch with you?"

"They did. The moment we heard about a man in military fatigues and a rifle attacking you it piqued our interest so we got our contact to do some digging. It was obvious this was Ben. It had him written all over it from what was said about the missing man. By the time we arrived, you'd already found him. The photo of him confirmed it was Ben, so we did some more digging and it was obvious you were the man to talk to about this."

"Not the police?"

"We don't do police. We do us," grunted Shorty.

"What does that mean?"

"It means we deal with things in our own way. Strictly off the books, undercover, and not always what you'd call sanctioned by the government." Phil hid behind his coffee and took a sip while his eyes never strayed from watching me.

Gummo smiled and said, "Relax, Max, we aren't here to hurt you. We're gutted we had to learn about Ben like this, but there was nothing we could do. He was already gone by the time we arrived. Killed right after you got smashed in the head. It was only the weirdness of what happened to you that made us look into things, but we came as soon as we could. Too late, but we did what we could."

"I'm still not following. How did you know it was Ben? There was nothing in the papers or online about it, so how did you find out?"

"Like I said," growled Phil, anger flashing across his face, "we know people and keep an eye on things. We got a call about the attack. They told us about a man named Ben who'd gone missing, and the description matched our guy. Bit crazy, as Ben was an absolute nightmare of a liar, but he never even bothered to change his name. Not his first name anyway. I guess a different surname was enough to put off our search, and it sure worked."

"But you knew him decades ago. You said so yourself. He would look very different."

"Not the physical description, the fact that he was an incorrigible liar. That had to be Ben. His nickname back in the day was Pants."

"Pants? I don't get it."

Shorty smirked and explained, "As in "Liar, liar, pants on fire,' like you used to say when you were a kid. Ben was awful for it. Always making stuff up. It was his thing. He got so into the nickname that he ended up believing half of what he made up. It got a bit much in the end, and was why he left. Bit of a mental breakdown, I'm afraid."

"Just like everyone else. All of us had issues, and had to get out eventually, but Ben was special. A real good guy and a great friend. We missed him a lot and always hoped we'd find him and see if he needed us. Now he does. He might be dead, but he needs us."

The others agreed, and they were obviously very close, but there was more I wanted to know. "What exactly did you guys do?"

"Cards on the table?" asked Phil, then drained his coffee.

"Sure."

"We can't, and won't, tell you. It was special ops, top secret, and we all signed the ton of paperwork they gave us promising never to disclose anything we did or any information about our team or even what we had for breakfast while in the employ of Her Majesty. Sorry, Max, but that's the way it is. We might not be active now, but we made a promise. And besides, we'd be in so much trouble if we told you that it really doesn't even bear thinking about." All three shuddered, and it was clear they took the work they'd done very seriously.

"Fair enough. But look, guys, I really think you've gone about this all wrong. I can tell you what I know, but it isn't much. You should have just come and asked me. If you're Ben's buddies, I would have shared."

"And get seen? No chance!" Phil crossed his arms and stared down at me, frowning. "Max, we have to keep our names out of this for obvious reasons. If we tip off the killer, we'll never get justice for Ben. We had to be covert. Yes, we snatched you, but no, nobody knows who did it. It's for the best this way."

"Then I suppose I better share what information I have, but like I said, it isn't much. Oh, and one more thing. You won't like it, and you really should have thought about it more before you took me."

"We thought about all possible contingencies," hissed Phil, nodding along with the others.

"You might think you did, but trust me, you overlooked one very important thing and boy are you going to pay for it."

"Was that a threat?" Phil laughed. "We can handle ourselves. We might be in our sixties, but you wouldn't want to mess with us.

"Of course it wasn't a threat! What I'm telling you is that nobody took my phone."

"I told you to do that!" Phil growled at Shorty.

"Forgot. It doesn't matter. He didn't know where he was going. Who could he call? What could he say? We were right there with him."

"He could have texted that he'd been kidnapped. This was meant to be hush-hush, not bring the cops down on us and mean no end of hassle."

"I didn't text. How could I? I was tied up, remember?"

"Yeah, of course he was," said Shorty with a grin at Phil.

"Then what're you on about, Max?"

"My phone can be tracked. It has one of those apps."

"So?"

"So, my folks are staying at the campsite, and the minute my mum turns up at my van and they can't find us, the next thing she'll do is check the app and then—"

We turned at the sound of a car crunching over the rough gravel road.

"Bugger," sighed Phil, rubbing at his head.

"Too late," I laughed. "Get ready for a world of pain like you've never experienced before."

"How bad can one mum be?" chuckled Phil. "We've dealt with terrorists, dictators, the nastiest people you can imagine.

"That's as maybe, but you've never dealt with Jill Effort. She makes those guys seem like naughty schoolkids in comparison. I warned you." I waved at Mum and Dad as they pulled up, already squabbling about Dad's parking and how slowly he'd driven.

Chapter 15

"…because you had the phone upside down, so of course I took the wrong turn!" Dad slammed the door shut then hurried around to the other side to open the door for Mum then help her out.

She kissed him on the cheek. "Thanks, love. You're still such a gentleman."

"Anything for my gal." He beamed at Mum, then crossed his arms, and continued where he'd left off. "You have to learn to hold the phone the right way up. It makes it impossible to navigate otherwise."

"I prefer a proper map. Not these stupid ones on phones."

"But you can't read a proper map either!" Dad protested.

"Ssh, we're in company. They'll think we don't know what we're doing." Mum waved merrily and shouted, "Hi, Max. It's me, Mum."

"And me, Dad." He grinned, then took Mum's hand and they wandered over, Mum crunching across the gravel in her high heels, her dress for the day an arresting black number with yellow polka dots, making me think of staring at the sun and getting the afterimage. Subtle, it was not, but at least it matched her bright yellow shoes and bandanna. She looked like a banana with bad spots, and the bright red hair certainly set off the yellow in a startling, utterly unforgettable way. She should have been arrested for her outfit, but woe-betide any cop who tried.

"This is what we should be worried about?" asked Phil with a smirk.

"You just wait," I said, grinning.

"Hey, guys. Decided to track me down, eh?"

"You weren't at Vee, and we searched the beach but you weren't there either. We were worried, so called, but there was no answer. You said you were going to the farm, but we knew something had happened as Tilly said you popped in to see her after." Mum crossed her arms, looking mad, then she smiled and dragged me in for a hug and I kissed her head.

"I'm fine. Sorry about not answering. It was on mute, and in my bag anyway. I couldn't get to it as these crazies kidnapped me and Anxious and tied my arms and legs. They put Anxious in a cage and he really didn't like it." I smiled smugly at the men, who were rather confused by me explaining so much, but I figured they deserved what was coming.

Mum sprang back, whirled on the men, and wagged a finger. "How dare you! You can't go around kidnapping my Max. And what about poor Anxious, eh? He's a delicate soul and you should know better. Well, what do you have to say for yourselves?"

Without giving the startled ex-soldiers a moment to gather their thoughts, Dad rolled up the sleeves of his white T-shirt, hitched up his Levi's, and demanded, "An explanation! I'll flatten the lot of you. Are you the killers? Is that what this is? Don't go thinking you can murder our Max, or Anxious. He'll bite your arses off. I'll clobber anyone who moves. Don't any of you dare look at my wife!"

Obviously, everyone turned to look at Mum, who smiled demurely and adjusted her headgear.

"Hey, now wait just one minute," said Phil, stepping forward.

From out of nowhere, Dad threw a wicked right hook and floored Phil, then stormed forward, stood over him, and hissed, "You move a muscle, mate, and I'll kick you in the knackers. You might be too old to have children, but unless you want to have to pee out of your bumhole you better stay still."

"Dad, I don't think peeing from your bum is a thing, no matter how hard you kick him. You can relax. They aren't going to hurt us."

"Oh, well that's alright then," said Dad happily, then reached out a hand to help Phil up. He took it rather cautiously, then let Dad haul him to his feet. Dad brushed Phil down, then turned to the other two men who stood in fighting stances and asked, "Anyone else want some?"

"If you weren't Max's family, that would have gone very differently," said Phil, moving his arm from behind his back and revealing a wicked knife almost as long as his forearm.

Gummo and Shorty both showed their own knives, grinning as they pointed to Phil. "He got you a good right hook there," laughed Gummo.

"Only because I let him." Phil turned to Dad and said, "The first one's free, but after that I fight dirty." To prove his point, Phil performed several quick jabs, then did a roundhouse that ended with his foot several millimetres from Dad's astonished face.

"I could take you," mumbled Dad, stepping back.

"Everyone calm down. Mum, Dad, it's great to see you, but you shouldn't have come. It might have been dangerous."

"It looks like it is." Mum whirled on Phil, got right up in his face, jabbed a finger at his nose, then demanded, "What do you want with my boy? What's the meaning of this? My Jack will clobber you all unless you explain right now. Oh, is that coffee? It smells nice. Can we have a cup? I'm parched."

"Me too," said Dad. "Milk in mine, but no sugar. I'm watching my weight." Dad patted his flat stomach then flexed his biceps for good measure, oblivious to the knives or the hard ex-military vibe oozing from the three utterly bemused men.

I caught Phil's eye and nodded. He nodded back, then wandered off in a daze with the others to do as they were told.

"Max, what's going on?"

"I'll explain in a minute, but there's no need to worry. They're friends of Ben."

"Oh, right, I see," said Mum, frowning, clearly not understanding at all.

Anxious barked shrilly, put out by the lack of attention, so Mum and Dad sat beside me and took turns making a fuss of him until the little guy was satisfied he was still the centre of the universe and everything revolved around him.

Dad leaned close to me and whispered, "Are you in danger? Blink once for yes, twice for no." He peered into my face and waited, and of course I had to blink. "So you are!" he gasped. "Jill, call the cops. Max is in danger."

"No, I'm not. I just had to blink. I'm fine. Shaken, but fine. These guys mean well, but they went about it the wrong way. I'll explain everything in a moment."

"You sure? Blink once for no, twice for yes, three times if it's an emergency."

"Dad, stop that. Everyone blinks, and you changed the rules anyway. Relax. Thanks for coming. I appreciate it. But you should have waited for me to come back. And will you please take that tracker off your phone? I'm a grown man."

"A grown man who got himself kidnapped," Mum reminded me. "Think what would have happened if we didn't turn up. Murdered, most likely. Left for the crows to peck your eyes out. Do you know what badgers do to corpses?"

"No. Do you?"

"Horrible things, probably. They look cute, but they have big teeth and really sharp claws. They need them for digging their burrows. I once saw one in the garden. It was —"

"Love, you're getting sidetracked," said Dad. "And badgers live in sets, not burrows."

"Am I? And sets of what? Never mind. Where was I? Oh yes, you could have been eaten by seagulls and—"

"Mum, I'm fine. You shouldn't have come, but it's great to see you both. How was the cottage? Did you sleep well?"

"It was lovely, dear. Very nice. The bed was a bit soft, but we managed. What about you?"

"Fine." I figured there was no point mentioning Tilly's late night appearance, but did explain that I'd heard Tony was let out and was innocent.

"So who did it if it wasn't him or his buddy? Think it was this lot?" whispered Dad, glancing over to the men who were clearly building up the courage to come back over.

"No, they're on the level. Look, here they come. Let them tell you everything." I smirked as they approached warily, figuring having to explain what they'd done, and why, to my folks, would be punishment enough.

And it was. Whilst Mum and Dad sipped their coffee, the guys tried to tell them what this was all about. As usual, neither of them were happy with the explanation, wanting more detail, descriptions of everything, including their homes, which they absolutely refused to do, and more info about what they planned to do, which seemed to leave them at rather a loss.

"Ha!" gloated Dad. "You don't know what to do, do you? That's why you stole our Max. You want him to do your dirty work for you. Well, let me tell you all something."

"Yes?" they sighed.

"Don't interrupt! Now I've lost my train of thought. Um, where was I? Ah, yes, that was it. Don't you expect our Max and his cute sidekick to solve this while you lot swan about kidnapping whoever you feel like. It ain't right and it ain't proper." Dad folded his arms across his chest and stared at the men, clearly impressed with himself.

"Look," said Phil warily, clearly expecting to be

interrupted. When he wasn't, he continued. "We came as soon as we could, figured it was best to take Max away discreetly, which may have been overboard, but we were in a rush. All we wanted was information from someone who seemed trustworthy. We read the wiki page and are impressed, so when we realised Max was on the case we, ahem, jumped at the chance to have a word."

"And now that you have?" I wondered.

The three friends huddled together, then broke apart after a quiet conversation and Phil said, "We'll leave it up to you. We think we'll come back to Shell Island with you and camp, but blend in and not draw attention to ourselves. That way we can mooch about and see what happens, but not get involved so much that the law comes asking us questions."

"You could have just done that anyway," said Mum.

"We did!" shouted an exasperated Gummo. "We just spent the last half hour telling you that. We've been there since yesterday, got right on it, but the three of us questioning Max would have been too obvious and anyone could have seen. We have to keep a low profile. We each have a tent separately so we can blend in and cover more ground, but it's such a massive place that it's impossible to know where to start."

"Let me get this straight," said Dad, frowning, and scratching at his stomach. "You did all this and your plan is to take Max back and leave him to solve this while you lot have fun camping? Gonna go crabbing too, are you? And what are you on about, keeping a low profile? You snatched them off the beach with who knows how many witnesses. The place might be crawling with cops and search parties because of what you did."

"Ooh, do they have crabbing?" asked Shorty. "I always loved doing that. Phil, do we have bacon to lure them?"

"No, we do not have bacon! Guys, this is serious."

"Just trying to lighten the mood," laughed Shorty.

"I've had enough," I sighed, using the warm granite

slab to shove off and stand. "I'm leaving. We're leaving," I told my folks.

"Too right we are. This place is creepy." Mum shivered, and hugged Dad for warmth, but more than that I think she was genuinely concerned about this weird situation.

"Look what you did to my wife," hissed Dad. "You frightened her."

"I am not frightened." Mum remained with her arms around Dad; he hugged her tightly and glared at the others.

"We honestly didn't mean to upset anyone," said Phil. "This is all for Ben."

"Give me a break. It's admirable you want to find out what happened to your friend, but to say you didn't want to upset anyone is laughable. You terrified me and Anxious. Any one of you could have explained on the beach or anywhere. This was dumb." Suddenly, a realisation hit, and I spun back to them and asked, "Wanted to relive the glory days, eh? Bored with your lives and couldn't wait to do something you were trained for, is my guess. Am I wrong?"

All three shifted about, avoiding my gaze, then one by one they admitted that maybe they had got carried away and that they should have taken a softly, softly approach rather than coming in hard like they had.

"Max, we're sorry. You're right," said Phil. "Our lives are mundane, normal, although we go off into the wilds regularly and camp, go for hikes, that kind of stuff, but yeah, we did lose the plot a little." They laughed nervously, looking sheepish, but at least it made more sense now.

"Seriously, you're laughing?"

The smiles vanished and they hung their heads, suitably chastised.

"We're really sorry," said Gummo. "I know this is no excuse, but it's impossible to explain what it's like after the army. Heck, we've been out for twenty years and we still find it hard to adjust. Not just regular army, and believe me, that's hard enough on a lot of men and women, but when you did what we did, lived how we did, then maybe you'd understand why we got carried away. We've tried paintball, we've tried getting locked in rooms to solve mysteries, and we've even been bodyguards and bouncers. Phil here was a cage fighter for five years, but even that didn't cut it."

"Nothing does," grunted Phil.

"What on earth did you do? I get that it was special ops, but what kind?"

"What's special ops?" asked Mum.

Dad held her hands now she'd calmed down a little, mostly because she wanted to hear about the gossip, and told her, "It's when men abseil down the sides of buildings and kill terrorists or free hostages. Go behind enemy lines via the sea in the middle of the night wearing nothing but their budgie smugglers with a knife between their teeth and kill an evil dictator. That kind of thing."

"That sounds like fun," beamed Mum.

"It was absolutely awful," laughed Phil.

"A real nightmare," agreed Gummo.

"And we loved every foul minute of it," sighed Shorty. "It's who we were, what we stood for, and who we still are. None of us can shake it off, and it gets to you, you know? We've never lived normal lives, have no other friends or partners. Nobody can stick around for long because they don't get it. We have to roam, go off for days, weeks, sometimes months at a time. Totally alone, just so we're no bother. But we always have each others' back."

"Always," agreed Phil. "It's been the one constant in our lives. Look, we apologise again, and it was dumb, but we thought we were doing the right thing when really all we were doing was reliving the past and playing at being soldiers. Utterly dumb."

"Sorry I was so harsh on you," I said. "I can't imagine the life you had, but I'm beginning to understand. I'm amazed none of you became vanlifers like me. That would have helped scratch the itch you seem to have."

"We tried it," admitted Shorty. "But we all get up at

least three times in the night for a pee and it was a total pain. Camping's easier as you can just poke your—"

"I think I get it," I laughed. "But surely you could get a portable toilet or use a bottle?"

"We tried all that, but truth be told we're getting on in years and have gone soft. We like to garden, and get the shopping delivered, and have a nice long shower in the morning. See, total softies."

"That is lame," agreed Dad amiably. "Even we stay in caravans and motorhomes now and then to visit Max. You should hear my Jill in the night when she gets up for a pee. It's like sleeping under a waterfall." Dad chuckled as he turned to Mum, but when he saw her face he took a hurried step away.

With a face like thunder, Mum insisted, "I do not make a noise when I pee. And a lady does not get up in the night. She holds it until the morning. You say sorry."

"Sorry," said Dad hurriedly. "You do not get up in the night for a pee, and it is not like someone's running a tap on low, and you never wake me, and if you did, I would never cover my head with a pillow even though I can still hear you."

"There you go then," said Mum, seemingly satisfied.

Dad wiped his brow, leaned in to me, and said, "That was a close one. Good job your mother never understood sarcasm."

"Yes, and you're always so great at picking up the subtleties and knowing when someone's being sarcastic."

"I know. I'm ace at it," he said seriously.

"Um, it's been great meeting you," said Phil after an awkward moment of silence, "but maybe we should be heading back now?"

Everyone agreed that was a good idea. I was starving hungry, having foregone breakfast, and desperate for another coffee, but it could wait, as what I wanted more than anything was to be left alone to process this and have a think about what to do next.

We said our goodbyes, then everyone piled into their respective vehicles. Anxious and I went with my folks, obviously, and Dad followed the guys back to the campsite, utterly incredulous that we were only ten minutes away as it had taken him and Mum half an hour to find me.

Once through the entrance, the others parked, then one by one they exited the Land Rover and went their separate ways, acting like they didn't know each other. It seemed like an odd thing to do to me, but I guess it was keeping them happy and they were reliving their past as much as anything. Dad dropped me at my place then he and Mum returned to the cottage as Mum needed to finish getting ready as apparently Dad had rushed her this morning and she wasn't quite spruced-up enough for the day yet.

I put the kettle on immediately, Anxious went for a sleep inside Vee, and once I'd made a cuppa I settled in my chair and gradually began to relax. What a morning. What a scare. But how sad that these men who thought the world of each other and Ben had been apart for so long. Ben could have had a very different life with them around, but he'd chosen to break free from them for some reason, and I could only speculate as to what that might have been.

Maybe he didn't want to be reminded of his past. Maybe it hurt too much. Or maybe he just plain didn't feel about them how they did about him. Whatever the reason, he'd chosen to live a life apart from all that haunted him, and it was only now that it had finally caught up with him. It seemed more likely than ever that whoever had murdered him was to do with his past, and the sooner I got to the bottom of that the sooner this would be solved.

Chapter 16

It took an age for me to come down from the stress of the morning. I don't think I'd ever been as scared in my entire life, certainly not about my own safety. I was also rather hyper—the two strong coffees might not have been such a great idea, but I'd needed it to calm my nerves.

It was tough to shake off such a wild morning, yet the fact I'd been kidnapped and survived left me out of sorts and both calm yet twitchy. Anxious could have died. I could have died. I thought that we would. When you face your own mortality and believe you'll lose your best buddy right before your eyes, it has a profound effect. Nobody is infallible, everyone can die without a moment's notice, and there truly is no bottom to the despair you can feel when confronted with the end.

Yet I was chuffed with myself because I'd handled what I'd believed to be the end of my life with more dignity and stoicism than I'd have imagined. My main concern was for the little guy, as he hadn't chosen to get involved in any of this, was just tagging along, trusting I had his back, and look what had almost happened. I felt awful. Anxious was pure and innocent like no human being could ever be, and trusted me implicitly. I had to be more careful moving forward, as there was no way I could bear to lose him. The poor fella had now been locked in a campervan cupboard, snatched from a walk and put in a crate, and had done nothing more wrong than wanting to play and maybe get the occasional treat.

What was I to do? How could I keep him safe? And myself? Keeping an eye out and always being aware of my surroundings wasn't enough. The guys proved that earlier. All I could do was try my best, keep my head down, and be mindful. Easier said than done when you're on the hunt for a killer. Leaving was always an option, but I felt too involved to do that. Although I hadn't known Ben for more than a few minutes near the end of his life, I still felt like I owed the man. Hearing from his old army buddies made me more certain than ever that I was doing the right thing by doing whatever I could to bring his killer to justice.

Ben was a broken man seen from the outside, but I wasn't so sure that was the truth of the matter. He cut ties with his crew for good reason, and maybe that reason was simply that he no longer wanted to think about his old life and begin anew living exactly how he wanted without anything holding him back. It made sense, and even his buddies understood the attraction of severing ties and living unencumbered by what was clearly a very difficult past.

Why was Russell murdered too? What was the connection? Why be so brazen when it came to killing the men? Neither served together and didn't know each other back in the day, but had become friends in later life. That and being military men was the only connection I'd discovered so far, but it didn't mean there wasn't more to their friendship. Maybe Russell had uncovered something in the time between us talking and his death. Maybe he'd done something that caused the killer to strike again.

What?

Scratching at my beard, I realised I had to take a break from thinking about any of this. My head was swimming, I was a mess of emotions, and on top of everything else I was absolutely famished. Time for lunch. That would calm me down and give me some energy rather than relying on caffeine which was making me jittery.

With familiar butterflies in my stomach that always happened when I thought about preparing a meal, I smiled as I rose then stood before my outdoor kitchen, mulling over my options and performing a mental checklist of what I had in the storage boxes and cupboards. I decided I needed something comforting and filling, but nothing too adventurous, so settled on scrambled eggs as they were quick to cook, filling, and super tasty if I made the extra effort.

I fried off onions, then added diced peppers, thinly sliced mushrooms, asparagus tips as a treat, then whisked up the eggs and added them to the pan before sprinkling Maldon sea salt and coarsely ground black pepper and turned the heat down low. The secret to good eggs, be they fried, scrambled, or an omelette, was to not mess with it too much. That way always led to them sticking to the pan, but if you started with a hot pan, always well-oiled or buttered, they wouldn't stick.

While the eggs cooked through until firm but still soft, I heated another pan and warmed through two oat wraps, a staple for me and imported from Staffordshire because you couldn't get them in Wales. Once everything was about ready, I mixed up the eggs properly to scramble them, then added half onto each oat wrap and grated cheese over the top, a very mature Cheddar that gave it a real punch. Then I folded them over, added a dash of hot sauce, and sat with a huge plate of food that made my mouth water and my eyes the same.

This was the life. Simple, good food done properly. A true taste sensation with no fuss but all the flavour. I tucked in eagerly, savouring every mouthful, and felt better immediately. Why did cooking always have this effect on me, I wondered? Because I was good at it, enjoyed the process, and I supposed it was my meditation. When I cooked, I focused like a laser beam and let everything else fade away. It was a solace and a comfort. More than just a hobby, but a true passion. Everyone needed something in their life they got excited about, right? Something to focus on, try to improve on, and to actually enjoy doing for the sake of it.

By the time I'd finished, I'd come to several

decisions. I would not tell Min about the kidnapping yet or she'd be sick with worry. I would do my best to get justice for Ben and Russell, and I would try to relax and not think the world was out to get me.

"Why was I sent here?" I asked myself as I hung the tea towel on the line to dry. I hadn't had the time to really think about it, but surely it had to be tied up with what happened? Didn't it? The slip of paper I'd found in my shirt pocket had Shell Island written on it, and was why I'd come here. Somebody had wanted me to make the trip. What did they know? Were they the killer? Why would they want me here?

It was vexing and utterly annoying. A mysterious note directing me to visit this beautiful place, but nothing more. Had the author known something bad was going to happen so wanted me here to help find out who it would be, or did they have an ulterior motive? It was clearly linked, and I had to find the answer. I crept into Vee, leaving Anxious to rest and recover, and pulled out the note from the drawer then took it outside and studied it while I sat in my chair.

What was it about the way the letter l was written, with that curl at the bottom that rose too high, making it look almost like a u? Why was that familiar? Was it something I recognised? The answer hit me and I shook my head in wonder at how I'd overlooked the blindingly obvious. This was no huge mystery to be solved. It had been staring me in the face all along!

"Mum!" I hissed.

"Yes, love?" she asked as she and Dad entered the gazebo. They were holding hands and looking rather flushed, and I noted that Dad's hair was mussed, not like him at all.

"Alright, Max?" Dad beamed at me, then kissed Mum's cheek and she blushed as she giggled.

"What have you two been up to?" I asked, regretting asking before the words were even out of my mouth.

"We had a lie down because we were exhausted

after that nonsense earlier, then your dad got quite frisky so we—"

"No, I do not want to know. Do not tell me."

"You did ask, Son," sniggered Dad.

"I know, and I regret it already. Look, I need to ask you something, Mum. You know when you write your name and—"

"Jill, you mean?" she asked, frowning.

"Yes, that's your name. Why would you ask me that?"

"Because you said did I know when I write my name."

"Max, are you feeling okay?" asked Dad. "You did just ask your mother that."

"Yes, I know what I said, but Mum interrupted before I could finish my sentence." I took several deep breaths, knowing I should be used to this by now, but once again shocked by their ability to derail the simplest of conversations. "Mum, when you write Jill, you always do the ls with a curl up. It's not something I've seen for years, but I suddenly recalled it."

"Yes, dearie, I suppose I do. But not just when I write my name, but for all ls. It's how I write."

"Then how do you explain this?" I whipped out the paper and held it up.

Mum blanched, Dad coughed then let go of her hand and suddenly found the ground very interesting. It was all the confirmation I needed, but I wanted her to admit it. I waited, knowing she couldn't stand the silence for long.

"Fine, it was me. I wrote it. I put it in that old shirt of yours, knowing you'd find it eventually, as Min told me she was going to cut the sleeves off. She brought it with her, didn't she, to the last place, along with some of your other things we found at home? We hoped you'd come here next, and you did." Mum beamed, like she was proud of herself, but Dad kept his mouth shut and his eyes averted.

"You set me up? You put the note in my pocket, but

never told me? I explained that I was worried about finding it, but you never said a word? Why not?"

"We thought it would be a fun mystery for you. We wanted to see how long it would take you to figure it out. It took you ages, and to be frank we were rather disappointed," she accused, jabbing a finger at me like this was my fault.

"Because you swore you knew nothing about it. I trusted you."

"And we feel bad, Son," mumbled Dad. He turned to Mum and said, "See, I told you we should have told him. Especially after the murders."

"But we wanted to come. We both agreed it would be lovely to see Shell Island. We've always wanted to visit." Mum took a step to Dad then peered up at him. He made the sensible decision and backed away, silent.

"So you set me up? I can't believe you two. Mum, I asked you about the note, but you said you were as in the dark as me."

"I know, and I'm sorry. We thought it would be a bit of fun. We never expected there to be a murder."

"I did," said Dad happily. "There usually is. Max, it was done with the best of intentions. We thought it would be nice to meet up, and we fancied a break. Rather than just ask you, your mother came up with this madcap idea."

"It was not madcap, and you said it was a great idea!"

"Maybe," he muttered. "We should have told you. We apologise."

We turned to Mum, who smiled and asked, "What?"

"I'm waiting for you to apologise properly."

"Your father just did."

"And?"

"And what?" Mum frowned, and picked at Dad's T-shirt like it was dirty, which it wasn't.

"You need to say it too."

"Fine," she huffed. "I'm sorry. It was silly, and I should have owned up. There, happy now?"

"I suppose. Don't do it again. But you guys turned up, saying it was because you got a call from the hospital."

"We did get the call, but we were already on our way once we heard you were here. You should have told us you were coming."

"I'm an adult. Sometimes I call and tell you where I'm off to next, other times I don't. I'm free to do what I choose."

"Course you are, love, but you should still tell us. So we don't worry." Mum patted Dad's stomach, like she was checking it was still flat, then came and kissed my cheek to show there were no hard feelings on her part.

"I never thought about it at the time, but when I was in the hospital you turned up really fast. This was why? You were already coming?"

Mum grinned.

I couldn't help it, and kissed her back then hugged her. She might have been absolutely mad, just like Dad, but they were my parents and I could never stay cross at them for long.

"At least now one mystery is solved. It's been really bugging me, so I'm glad you owned up."

"What's the latest?" asked Dad, changing the subject. "We had our lunch, figuring you'd want some time alone, but have you come up with anything?"

"Not yet, no. I can't figure out the connection between Ben and Russell, and am not even sure there is one, but regardless of that, the only thing I can think to do now is go and visit Russell's parents and see if they have any insight. I've already been to the farm, so I'm not sure what else there is."

"Ugh, a stinky farm! Imagine if I'd gone in these shoes. Pass." Mum pulled a face and snorted, like she could smell the manure.

"We'll hang here, Max, and leave you to do your

thing in peace. How about we go for fish and chips in Barmouth this evening? My treat. Get us away from here and have a nice evening. Maybe a stroll on the beach too?"

"That sounds perfect. I'll be back later this afternoon and we'll catch up then. Stay out of trouble."

"Us?" asked Mum, shocked.

"Yes, you two. Take it easy, enjoy the trip you've seemingly been planning for a while, and make the most of the sea air."

Anxious woke and came out to say hello, then after he'd had a fuss my folks left, leaving me to finish cleaning up a few things. I sat for a while, despairing of my parents' antics, but pleased it was nothing sinister behind the note, then got a few things together, but couldn't seem to drum up much enthusiasm for a drive.

The day had been too much for me, I admitted, so rather than leave, I set out the bed in Vee then had a lie down with my best buddy. It was exactly what I needed, and after a few minutes I felt myself calming, and soon drifted off a little less apprehensive than I'd been all day, but not as relaxed as I'd have liked.

The nap did me good, and when I woke, I felt so much better. I hadn't realised how exhausted the ordeal had made me, but it was no surprise and I should have known better than to plan a trip before getting some rest.

Anxious woke when I moved, so I sorted out the bed then checked everything was in order before setting off. I wasn't sure what to do about telling Tilly any of this, but felt I owed it to her, so rather than going into reception and trying to explain, I called her. She answered on the second ring, and said it was fine to talk as she was on a break, so I explained about my morning, but put a different slant on it, saying I'd bumped into some of Ben's old army buddies.

She had nothing of interest to share, though, and had been busy with work but hadn't seen or heard anything strange. She was rather annoyed about that, and the lack of a police presence now the bodies had been cleared and the teams had been in, and asked if this was normal. Shouldn't a detective be wandering around asking questions until the case was closed?

I explained that every detective worked in a different way, and there was always a lot of paperwork involved along with things that could be checked online, but that yes, this was a rather unique way of going about things. It was hard for me to say too much, though, as I hadn't even met the detective in charge and it seemed like it was going to remain that way. I hung up with neither of us any the wiser about events, but both promising to get in touch if anything did come up.

Anxious and I took a very short walk, which we both felt nervous about at the start, but we got into our stride and ended up enjoying ourselves. In fact, it was just what we needed to clear our heads and stop such a simple act filling us with dread.

Back at Vee, we piled in, buckled up, and intended to head away from Shell Island and up into the surrounding hills to see if we could finally get some information about Russell and his past, or any information that might help solve this peculiar and downright disconcerting series of crimes.

Chapter 17

In the end, I decided to stop at the car park and speak to Tilly in person. I'd missed out plenty on the phone, so knew a face-to-face was in order. I owed her that much. Inside reception, I hesitated for a moment, still in two minds about what to tell her.

"Max, there is something, isn't there?"

"Yes, but it's a wild one and doesn't help us figure this out."

"Tell me," she insisted.

"Okay." I explained about our morning kidnap, rather than what I'd said on the phone about meeting some of Ben's old army buddies, trying to make it sound less traumatic that it had been, but judging by her wide eyes and shocked expression, I failed miserably.

"They actually kidnapped you and took you to the quarry? That's crazy."

"I know, and I didn't want to worry you or get the police involved. They seem like nice enough guys. A little unhinged to come up with such a dumb plan, but I think their hearts are in the right place. You won't report them, will you?"

"Not if you don't want me to, no. They wouldn't tell you what they did in the army though?"

"They were completely vague about it and refused to go into detail. They looked for Ben for years, and have had feelers out ever since. I got the impression they know a lot of people in various police or private security positions, so can call in favours if they need to. But nobody had heard a peep out of Ben until it was too late. They came to help their friend, but are as in the dark as us."

"So what do we do now? What next? I haven't got anything that can help. I've been asking around but nobody saw or heard anything strange regards Ben, just the usual stuff about seeing him here and there, listening to him tell tall tales, and no idea who would want to hurt him."

"What do you know about the farm and Willow and Owen? It's a weird place, right?"

"Everyone knows them. They were the talk of the town for years. Everyone loves to gossip, and what with him being twenty years younger it was a real shock when they got together. But they seem happy and are kind people."

"The hoarding goes back a long way, so I hear."

"Used to be even worse. His dad was mad for machines and used to collect tractors. It slowly got to the point where the fields were overrun and Owen actually had a clear-out when he took over. But like father, like son, and now it's back to being in the terrible state you saw. Willow's lovely though. Really kind, and always smiling. Everyone likes her."

"She was very nice. Okay, I better get on. My folks are still here, and I promised to meet with them later. If I leave them alone for too long they'll get themselves into trouble."

"Unlike you," Tilly teased, laughing.

"Yes, unlike me," I said, mock-serious, then laughed along with her. "The difference being, they are always utterly oblivious to the trouble they are in, and merrily talk their way through it all and seem surprised when I tell them what happened."

"You love them a lot, don't you?"

"I really do. They've always been there for me, and I owe them everything. Even when I made a monumental mess of my life, and my ex-wife's, they stood by me. Sure, they told me off all the time, but I knew they'd always have my back."

"That sounds wonderful. I never had anything like that. Mum was always distant, there were a string of boyfriends but…"

"But what? You okay?"

"Yes, fine. It is what it is. Let's just say I never knew my father. He could have been anyone."

"At least you had Ben. He looked out for you, didn't he?"

"Actually, he really did. The moment I started work here he took me under his wing in his own mad way. Took care of me."

"Almost like he came here because you were here," I joked, but Tilly flinched and turned away and busied herself with the pamphlets. "I'll speak to you later?" I asked, as she obviously wanted to change the subject.

"Yes, that will be fine. Hopefully, there will be something we can do."

Out in the car park, I paused to consider Tilly's reaction to what I'd said. Could Ben have come to be close to her? Was there something going on? Was he her father? Did she know? Did the ages add up? They could, but what was I getting at here? Carried away, that's what I was getting.

After returning to the van, I stood for a while outside Vee with the doors open to keep it cool inside and thought about the morning and the strange farm. It was a dead end, but I was intrigued by the couple and their strange way of life. How had Ben managed to touch the lives of so many people, yet nobody knew a thing about him? Why Russell too?

"You utter idiot!" I shouted at myself, shaking my head. "Will you never learn?"

Anxious came tearing from Vee and barked, scanning for trouble. Fair play to the little guy, even after everything he'd been through he had my back without hesitation.

"It's okay, there's nothing wrong. Apart from with me. How did I not see this all along, Anxious? What a fool I've been. What a fool everyone's been. I've been so obsessed with Ben that I didn't pay enough attention to what this has been about from the start. Better late than never, I suppose. What shall we do now? How to get this figured out? Russell knew everyone in the area and lived here his whole life apart from when he was in the army, but who should we talk to? Who had the motive? He might be the answer to all of this and we haven't been diligent enough in looking into him or his past. So stupid."

I called Tilly and asked her as many questions as I could think of, deciding to share my thoughts and that possibly, just possibly, we'd been looking at this all wrong. What if it wasn't Ben that the killer had been after at all? What if it was Russell, and the killer made a mistake so came back to assassinate the right man? It made sense, and the more I thought about it, and the more Tilly talked, the more I grew confident I might be on to something. Unless, of course, it was Tilly. Long-lost daughter of either Ben or Russell? Granddaughter? She'd acted super weird when I suggested Ben came because of her, but wouldn't it make more sense that it was Russell who was her father and stayed close to keep an eye on her but she found out and lost the plot?

Tilly answered all my questions, though, and by the end of the conversation she'd put my mind at ease and I couldn't believe it was her who had committed such a heinous crime. She certainly wouldn't mistake one man for the other, unless killing Ben was so everyone would focus on that. A decoy?

No, surely not.

By the time I hung up, I was more confused than ever. The list of suspects seemed to keep growing, yet I kept returning to Tilly, most likely because she was closest to everyone involved. But what about Tony or the guy he was with just before Russell was murdered? What about any of the other workers at the campsite, or his supposed friends? Maybe it was them and they nabbed me to check what I knew. If I'd told them I was on to something, maybe they would have never let me go.

I had to speak to Russell's family and see what light they could shed on this. There was nobody else I could think to talk to. After this, I was out of ideas, and worried that I was almost out of time too. If this wasn't solved soon, then I felt it never would be.

Reluctantly, and feeling tired to my core, I made up my mind to pay Russell's family a visit right now rather than keep procrastinating. I kept finding excuses, mainly talking to Tilly, but it was now or never.

With the address loaded into my phone, I set off yet again, with Anxious napping the entire way, making me jealous.

It was a short trip to the rather plain bungalow surrounded by other nondescript homes on a new housing development, one of the ones where they built a variety of homes both large and small, expensive and somewhat more affordable, to encourage a mixing of the generations and people from different social backgrounds. All very laudable in one regard, yet clearly pitting people against each other in a very obvious way, as it was clear who had money and who didn't by the size of the buildings. What the answer to such an issue could be I had no idea beyond everyone living in identical houses, but clearly that wouldn't work either.

The front garden was small but immaculate. A square of manicured grass with pansies and pelargoniums lined up like soldiers. Hanging baskets dripped with purple lobelia, almost as overpowering as the scents from tubs of white and orange lilies beside the white UPVC front door. It reminded me of Mum and Dad's description of their old place before they bought the house I grew up in, and made me smile instantly as I rang the bell and the chime went off inside.

Anxious yawned beside me; the poor guy was done

for.

An elderly lady using a walking stick, her shoulders hunched and back crooked, answered with a weary smile and said, "Hello? What can I do for you?"

"Hello. My name is Max, and I'm so sorry to disturb you at this time of mourning, but I wanted to offer my condolences."

"Thank you. That's very kind. How did you know my son?"

"I'm afraid I hardly knew him, but I was the one who found him. I also found his friend, Ben. I was hoping to have a word with you and your husband, if that's okay? Would that be convenient?"

"Now?" she glanced back into the house down the narrow hallway where I could hear a radio blaring, then sighed and said, "Yes, you better come in."

"Anxious, wait here please."

"It's okay, he can come in. We adore dogs and he's so cute. Does he like a cuddle?"

"He sure does. Maybe once you're sitting down he can have a fuss?"

"That sounds lovely." She seemed to perk up at the thought of that, so hobbled down the hallway, leaving me to remove my boots then follow into a rather small but very neat and clean kitchen where a man was sitting at a small round pine table doing a crossword.

"We have a visitor," she informed him.

"Who is he?" he asked, staring from his wife to me.

"Name's Max," I said. "Sorry for your loss."

"Thanks," he grunted.

After I was offered tea, which I refused, we settled at the table and Anxious carefully got into Irene's lap and flopped upside down much to her amusement, and there he remained for the whole conversation having his tummy rubbed while we discussed things. Malcolm was the quiet type, hardly said a word, and I suspected it wasn't just because of his sadness, but he was always like that. Irene, on the other hand, was a real chatterbox and hardly stopped for breath, so keen was she to share everything about her boy, even though he'd died at the age of fifty-six.

What I gleaned from the conversation was that Russell had enlisted at seventeen, served for many years, but eventually left after a final tour in Afghanistan that had gone badly and left him utterly traumatised. He'd moved back home, then left when he got engaged, but it had gone wrong and when he separated from his partner he became a traveller before returning and settling in the area, refusing to move back into the family home.

Finally, his parents had sold the house and moved into the new-build bungalow as it suited their health requirements better, but Russell still refused to live with them. He visited every week or two, but apart from that did his own thing, working odd jobs but mostly living off an army pension. They knew all about Ben, some from their son, some from friends and others in the area who picked up the gossip, but only as much as I'd heard from everyone else.

Russell was different, and spoke more openly about his time away, but refused to discuss what exactly had happened in Afghanistan. When it came to the subject of why anyone would want to hurt him, they both grew angry, saying their son was a good man and never did anything to deserve what happened. They could think of nobody he'd ever mentioned he had a cross word with, or anyone with a grudge.

"What about children?" I asked cautiously. "Did he have any children, or could he have a child he didn't know about?"

"No children," grunted Malcolm.

"Could there be a child he wasn't aware of?" I knew I was pushing things, but had to at least try to get an answer.

"Only his ex," said Irene. "She wasn't our kind of person, and we never saw eye to eye, but I suppose if she'd had a child it would be young now, maybe fifteen or less. I lose track of the timing."

"What about while he was in the army? Any girlfriends then?"

"Not that we know of, but he was away so much. Why do you ask?"

"Just trying to cover everything I can think of. I want to help."

"Why?"

"Because I was there, and because I feel like I owe it to Ben and Russell to uncover the killer."

Both tried their best to think of anything, but there was nothing they could say that gave me any new insight, and I left after promising I would keep trying. Part of me felt like this had been a wild goose chase, but I knew that this was how you figured stuff out. You kept talking to people and something would fall into place.

I was definitely getting that little nagging sensation at the back of my neck, and hints of the truth lurking in my head. Revelations not quite formed, but slowly cohering and soon I would have the answer I searched for.

We headed back to the site. My thoughts swirled, wisps of answers drifting far back in my head then swept away before I could reach out and grab hold and tug them to the fore. Something was there, though, becoming more insistent, and I knew it would only take a final seemingly unimportant event or word for everything to make sense.

At the entrance, several cars were queuing to leave, the energetic bloke manning the barrier always keen to have a chat with those in no hurry. He was talking to a man leaning out of his car window, laughing at something, when I heard the familiar revving of the quad engine that was always doing the rounds of the site. It skirted past the line of cars and the driver nodded. The barrier was raised for him and he drove through with a salute that the security guard mimicked.

We pulled up in the car park and I frowned as I looked back at the exit, the quad now gone, the driver with his helmet that covered his head and face presumably racing off to either go home for the evening or to another job. Anxious wasn't keen on yet another visit to reception, so as I was parked in the shade I left him in Vee with the windows open and promised I'd be quick. He grunted, then closed his eyes, happy as only a content pooch could be.

"Any news?" asked Tilly, smiling at a guest who had presumably just booked in.

"Nothing at Russell's parents." I nodded to the woman and held the door open as she left with an excited smile, clearly keen to begin her holiday.

"Shame. Were they very upset?"

"Very, but holding it together. It must be terrible to lose a child, no matter what age they are."

"The worst."

"Hey, I just saw that quad leave."

"Not a quad, it's an ATV really. It's legal to drive on the roads."

"You can drive all quads on the roads if they are licensed and insured, can't you?"

"Um, I guess." Tilly shrugged.

"And it looked like a quad to me. Sure, it had the cage for storage, but it's still a quad, isn't it?"

"Max, you're confusing me. Yes, I suppose it's a quad, but around here the larger ones that are used for campsites and what the farmers drive are called ATVs. I think it makes them feel more adventurous by calling them that. Owen always calls his an ATV. He loves that it's a tipper. Says it's easier for unloading wood and stuff he picks up around the other farms."

"Owen?" Something clicked in my head. "You're telling me that Owen, the Owen I went to see at the farm, with his wife, Willow, works here and can drive in and out without even stopping at the exit? That he's around often?"

"Course he is. He's worked here for years and years. Since before he was even old enough to drive legally. He used to come with his dad apparently."

"Tilly, you never thought to mention that? He has

that quad with space in the back for loads of gear, often covered by a tarp, with a helmet on so you can't see his face, and he comes and goes as he pleases?"

"Max, what's got into you? I assumed you knew. Didn't we talk about it?"

"No, we did not. What's his job here? I assumed it was someone I see driving around in the 4x4s, selling wood, checking on things, or on that huge ride-on mower. That's him too?"

"Now and then, yes. He uses the mower sometimes, but usually he's in the ATV. It's his. He does the rounds a few times a week, sometimes every day. Depends what he finds. You wouldn't believe this, but occasionally people up and leave and don't take their tents with them. If they get damaged, sometimes people abandon them. It's terrible. So now and then he's here every day, sometimes multiple times a day. He drops off firewood in the hard to get to spots, helps pull out people who get stuck in the sand, or if it's muddy, and even clears up the beaches. Plus, he helps take the boats to the water. People are always coming with trailers for their boats and he uses the ATV to get them to the jetty. Max, why are you hopping about?"

"Don't you get it? Ben worked up there, Russell, too, and Owen has free rein to drive about without ever being questioned or stopped at the exit, and I assume it's the same when he arrives?"

"Of course it is. He works all over the area doing stuff for other sites and farms, like I said. How do you think he's managed to collect so much stuff? He takes it away for people, but rather than scrap it or sell it most ends up back at his. He's always tinkering with machines, saying he can fix anything, but he loses interest and most of it rusts away at his place."

"So nobody would bat an eyelid if they saw him driving around no matter what time of day or night? Do the police know? When we were at the farm, they said the police had been, but neither mentioned being questioned about his work."

"I'm not sure if they know or not. Max, so many people work here. It's a huge operation with loads of staff. We've got like ten mowers or something silly, and who knows how many people clearing bins, the cleaners, working in the shop, the pub, here, and all over. It's amazing it runs so smoothly."

"And Owen's part of that? He doesn't have set hours or tasks?"

"He comes at all hours. Like I said, it depends on what the work is he's doing." Tilly stared at me hard, frowning, and I waited for the penny to finally drop. "Oh!" she gasped, her hand going to her mouth, eyes wide.

"Yes, oh indeed. Tilly, how well do you know Owen? I didn't speak to him for long, it was mainly his wife, but he seemed like a nice guy. What's his deal?"

Tilly shrugged like there wasn't much to say. "He's a farm type. Lived up there his whole life. Fell in love with Willow despite the age difference, and his folks thought it was the right time to let him have the farm when they were getting married. He works hard, is always doing something, and is a nice guy. He looked out for Ben. They both did. We all did."

"Never any issues with him? Any bother here?"

"Absolutely not. Max, you can't be serious? It couldn't be him."

"It certainly could. He never mentioned that he worked here. He can come and go whenever. Nobody takes any notice. I bet he's not even remembered as it's like seeing the postman walking down the street. Something so familiar that you could easily forget if you saw him or not."

"I guess." Tilly wrung her hands and lost focus, then slowly looked up and asked, "Why would he do it though? Why on earth would he be so cruel?"

"I don't know. But I intend to find out. When is he due back?"

"No idea. He doesn't have set hours, just bills for his time once a month. He has a contract to keep things in order and he usually checks to see if he has to make any deliveries to the pitches, but he's his own boss. Sometimes every day, sometimes he doesn't come for days, and other times he's back and forth multiple times. Depends on the work."

"Then we need to have a serious think about this. Obviously, there's no proof, not yet, but I'm going to go back to my pitch and try to think this through properly."

"What should I do?"

"If he comes back, just be careful. Act like nothing's wrong. Maybe there isn't, but be cautious."

"I will. I hope it wasn't Owen. He's such a nice guy."

"See you soon."

Chapter 18

Anxious was still dozing, but woke when I opened the door. He closed his eyes quickly, feigning sleep, and I chuckled as I started Vee then drove back to our pitch. Although time was getting on, I had to rest awhile, so made a coffee, settled, and did my best not to think about anything at all and let my brain work its way through things without me being consciously involved. It's easy to overthink and get yourself into a real muddle, but I'd found that if I let go, relinquished control and trusted in my innate abilities, everything worked its way out eventually.

The coffee hit the spot, and I was relaxed by the time I'd finished. Slowly, I replayed the encounters I'd had so far, letting different scenarios and possibilities play out, hitting dead end after dead end until something that flashed by and I almost missed caught my attention and I focused on it. On a name. On how this could have been pulled off. I had to be sure, and I wasn't, but Owen on the quad simply couldn't be ignored and so I formulated a plan that should see things come to a head soon enough.

Grinning despite the serious nature of the crimes, maybe feeling a little smug, too, I called Tilly and told her to spread the news that I'd told her I knew who killed Ben and Russell and I was going to do a big reveal on the beach at midnight.

"Why midnight?" she asked after I'd explained the rest of the plan.

"So it's dramatic, and so we can keep the danger to the guests at a complete minimum. Tell everyone who's involved in this that I'm a bit crazy if you want, but I'm going to tell everyone that turns up who the killer is and then we're going to go and get them and drag them to the police station. Tilly, you've got to be sure to tell people that I have evidence. That there's proof."

"So why wouldn't you just go to the police now if that's the case?"

"Because that's not how these things work. You have to do the big reveal. Like I said, tell everyone I've gone off my rocker and the cases always end with an impressive finale, so that's what I'm going to do before we go and get the killer and they're locked up for life. Can you do that?"

"If you're sure, Max. It sounds dangerous."

"It is," I admitted. "But remember what I told you about the plan. If this works how I think it will, then everything will be fine. We'll get this monster, then this will be over."

"But what about real proof?"

"Leave that to me. You trust me, don't you?"

"Of course I do. I know you didn't trust me though. I get it. You've been trying your best to figure this out, but we're friends, aren't we?"

"We are, and I'm sorry if you felt we weren't. You're right, I did suspect you, but things are different now. Can you do this?"

"I can, and I will. See you later!"

Smiling, I rinsed out my mug, gave Anxious his dinner, called my folks to arrange to collect them, then we drove over to the cottage for our big evening out.

It promised to be a real doozy.

Mum and Dad were understandably concerned about me being absent for most of the day, and made a point of pouting and looking upset, when the truth was that they'd had a lovely time going for walks, "hanging out in the bedroom" as Dad put it whilst squeezing Mum's bum, having a few drinks up at the bar, and relaxing in the sun. They even went for a paddle on the beach, with Mum, gasp, taking off her high heels again. She regretted it, of course, and complained that her feet had grown fat whilst out of her shoes and now it was hard to get them back on.

It was great to listen to their banter and faux moaning—life as normal, which I never tired of.

Dad and I hung out while Mum finished getting ready, which took as long as expected, much longer than she promised, but we were old hands at this now and knew the deal.

Once we were ready, I promised I would explain everything in Barmouth, so we headed off, excited to have an evening together and to relax and enjoy all the seaside had to offer. The drive didn't take long, and as I pulled into the car park the other side of the road from the beach, I was pleased to note how empty it was. It was still relatively early in the season and although busy in the daytime, the evenings were always quieter, so we wouldn't be waiting too long in any queues.

We hit the arcade first as Anxious loved the Coin Pusher, a machine that had him rolling two pence pieces down the little tracks with his nose, watching keenly as they toppled onto the trays. He whined when they didn't push off others and money would spit out of the bottom of the dastardly machines designed to feed your addictive personality traits to the max.

My folks were as excited as young children, both returning from the change machine loaded with coins so they could play in the arcade. They went straight at it on the Coin Pusher next to me and Anxious, hardly pausing to let one coin fall before slotting another into place. Within ten minutes they'd both lost a fiver and were grumbling about it being one big con, but Anxious held his cup full of money to their faces to prove that he was a much better player than them.

"Yeah, well, that's because you have a great sense of smell," grunted Dad, eyeing his windfall.

I let Anxious down onto the top of the machine and put a coin into place, then he nudged it with his nose and we both turned and grinned when money spewed from the bottom.

"It's all fixed!" Mum wailed, making a grab for the winnings.

"Oh no you don't. It's time to leave before you spend all your money. Come on, let's go for a wander then get dinner."

"And you can explain what's been going on today," said Dad, slapping Mum's hand away as she tried to steal Anxious' winnings.

"I will, I promise." I went and cashed in the coins for some larger ones, then met them outside.

It was still a beautiful day with the sun shining, everyone happy, and the gulls screeching. You couldn't beat the beach at this time of the day, but most didn't get the chance to experience it as they had to leave to get home. We had the luxury of being at the campsite, so could stay as late as we wanted.

Down on the incredibly long beach the tide was out, so it was quite a trek to the water, but great fun watching Anxious tear off and race about the place like he owned it. While he ran ahead, I explained about my visit to Russell's parents, apologising for not taking them along, then going into the final revelation when I spied Owen on his quad and Tilly told me about his erratic work schedule.

"So what's the plan, my smart son?" asked Dad, panic-combing his hair as he was so excited.

"We're going to get our assassin this evening. I told Tilly to spread the word I'm doing a big reveal at midnight, then we're going to confront the lunatic who killed two men."

"But won't they just deny it?"

"No, because I said I have proof. They'll have to act."

"And do you?"

"Nope," I grinned.

"Max, this is dangerous. They aren't going to turn up at midnight and let you point the finger at them, surely?" asked Mum.

"That's the plan."

Both frowned, confused, so I explained what I had in mind and what I assumed would happen, and they both grew concerned but said they trusted my judgement so would do whatever they could to help. With everything settled, we continued our walk, let Anxious play with the other dogs he met, and had a nice relaxing time. I still couldn't believe they'd tricked me into coming by leaving the note in my shirt pocket like that, but was glad they had as it was great spending time with them.

Suitably tired, we had a paddle then took a leisurely stroll back up the beach towards the small seaside town, the shops open late to cater to the tourists, the usual bucket and spade places busy despite the hour. Cafes and ice-cream kiosks were doing a roaring trade, and so was the chip shop, so we had to wait a while to get served. Once we did, we hurried back to the seafront, found a free bench, and sat, eager to sample the incredible looking fish and chips, the smell of salt and vinegar, crispy batter, soft fish, and perfect chips one of the true delights of the seaside.

We sat beside each other, with Anxious between Mum and Dad as he knew they were a soft touch, then tucked in. As expected, it was perfect. Piping hot, almost swimming in malt vinegar and salt, but the batter remained crispy as we were seasoned pros at this, so rested the fish on the fold over lid so it kept dry. The little guy was well-behaved, never pestered, and was rewarded generously for his immaculate behaviour.

By the time we'd finished, we were stuffed, and Mum downright refused to move, so I gathered up the cartons and paper and disposed of them with a slight waddle, then collapsed back onto the bench with a happy sigh.

"This is the life, eh, Son?" said Dad, beaming.

"Perfect," agreed Mum.

"A lovely evening. Thanks for being so understanding about today. It's been a whirlwind, but it was best to get out and speak to people and try to figure everything out."

"And you did. You worked it out. Are you sure?" asked Dad. "I mean, a hundred percent certain you have this solved?"

"I'm sure. I have no idea why, but I know who."

"Then we have your back," said Dad.

"Oh no you don't! You pair are staying well away from this. I don't want you getting hurt."

"We won't get hurt. We never get hurt," said Mum.

"I can't take the risk. I want you tucked up in bed at the cottage so I won't be distracted worrying about you. Please? For me?"

"We can't do that. You know what we're like, Max," said Mum. "No way can we stay away and miss the fun."

"Fun? It's catching a murderer."

"Exactly. What fun! What time do you reckon it will kick off? Should we just come back to yours and wait?"

I shuddered at the thought, and said, "That could be risky. We don't want to tip them off. Better to wait until the last minute and follow the plan. That way, we have the best chance of it working out." I explained what I'd arranged with Tilly, and they promised they would follow her lead if I let them get involved, so begrudgingly I agreed.

"Then it's a deal," said Mum with a smile. She looked down at her hands and frowned. I'd been anticipating this and came prepared; I handed her a few wet wipes so she could clean the grease off before it got onto her dress. She almost wept as she took them. "You're such a good boy looking after your mum like this."

"What about me?" asked Dad.

"Wipe them on your jeans," I laughed.

"You what!? These are classic Levi's 501s. You don't wipe your hands on them."

I handed him a fresh wet wipe with and wink and

he smiled.

Once our food had gone down enough to stand without discomfort, we decided another stroll would be nice, so walked along the promenade to burn off a few calories and watched the sun set. It was beautiful here. Yes, it was a rather dated seaside town that some would call old-fashioned, but that was the whole point, and the charm of the place. It was what people liked, what was familiar and relaxing, and Barmouth had one of the absolute best beaches around. Next to Aberdyfi and the beaches at Harlech it was one of my favourite places, although come to think of it, Portmeirion wasn't too far up the coast and an absolute must if you'd never been.

After a drink at a cafe, we headed back to the campsite to ready for the nighttime showdown. I dropped off my folks as I told them I had things to arrange, but in truth there was little I could do until the time got closer. The one thing I made sure to do was call Phil. He was with Gummo and Shorty, so I explained what my plan was. He wasn't impressed until I explained that I was relying on them to back me up, ensure nobody got hurt, and that it was vital they were ready.

They would be, he assured me, although he wasn't happy about the short notice I'd given them. I apologised, but in reality I had wanted to leave it until now so they wouldn't mess things up by getting too eager to proceed and trying to take things into their own hands.

Now it was a waiting game.

I drank a glass of wine, a small one, sorted out a few things around the van and in the kitchen, then settled down with a small fire to keep me company as Anxious was asleep on the bed the moment I folded it down. The fire allowed me to zone out, which was important as otherwise I'd be stressing about if I'd done the right thing, but as time got on I began to get antsy and had to pace around as the last thing I wanted to do was fall asleep or second-guess myself.

At eleven, I had one more thing left to do, so I

roused Anxious and for the next fifteen minutes I did my best to explain to him what he had to do, which involved him sniffing what I held out until he was familiar with the scent. To do this, we played an exciting game of me hiding it and him retrieving it for a lovely biscuit reward, which he had great fun doing.

It was now almost half past, so it was time. I'd told Tilly for everyone to meet at twelve, which meant the killer should arrive any moment, as no way would they wait until there was anyone else around. This was the real plan, not what Tilly told everyone else. Word of mouth would have spread to the farm, so any minute now I should hear the sound of a quad.

Right on cue, I caught the faint rumble of the engine before it cut out, but not before a light in the distance gave away the position of the vehicle. Then all was silent. I stoked up the fire, steeled myself, and waited for Anxious to give me the signal from his spot atop the dune. A single, staccato yip was all I needed, then he came tearing down to me and I handed over the biscuit. He'd caught the scent and the game was on.

I arranged the rather badly put together fake body I'd made while I waited in my chair, consisting of a pair of jeans and a jacket stuffed with clothes, a beach ball I'd picked up this evening for a head, with seaweed and a hat on top for good measure. I left my Crocs by the fire just to be sure it would pass for me. I stood back, inspecting my work, then frowned and shifted everything further under the gazebo so it was obscured in deeper shadow.

I paced a little, nodded my satisfaction that it would pass for someone sitting by the fire, then we retreated into the dunes and waited. Tilly was already there, and so were my folks, having done as they were asked and staying out of sight and even silent, which I'd known all along was a big ask from my parents, but they'd upped their game this time.

We said nothing, just nodded, then I lay down like them and we peered over the top of the dune and watched and waited.

It wasn't long before a dark figure in army camouflage and wearing a balaclava came creeping down the dune opposite from the road and sneaked towards the fire. They were approaching from the fire side, so would be partially blinded by the light, but off to one side enough to make a surprise attack. The figure paused, and cocked their head, then hunched over before getting down onto all fours and crawling ever so slowly towards "me".

We held our breath as the killer finally got close to the figure in the chair, then they leapt up, pulled the rifle from over their shoulder, took aim, and fired. Even with the silencer on I heard the dull sound of the weapon, but it was the *pfffft* of the beach ball head deflating that caused Anxious to bark in excitement and for Mum and Dad to titter like kids.

"Game's up!" yelled Dad as he leapt to his feet and raced after the startled would-be assassin.

Anxious refused to be left out and scrambled down the dune and bounded ahead of Dad.

"Dad, no! Anxious, come here!" I screamed, but in that instant my shouts were drowned out as a helicopter came *whoop, whoop, whooping* from across the island, search lights tracking across the sand then highlighting the killer and Dad and Anxious nearly upon their prey. Sand blew everywhere, the gazebo was buffeted and I worried it would snap but it held fast. However, the same could not be said for my chair which tumbled end over end as the fake Max was blown away into the dunes. The collapsible fire pit thankfully got blown away from our pitch, which was a hair-raising moment until the coals faded.

As the helicopter spun in a wide arc and the spotlight held surprisingly steady on the scene below it, I was already halfway down the dune with Tilly by my side and Mum wailing for us to wait for her.

"Where did the helicopter come from?" shouted Tilly.

"I have no idea, but they could have blown everything if they'd been a few seconds earlier."

In the confusion, the gunman had managed to dodge Anxious who had wasted valuable seconds looking up at what to him would have been an utterly confusing spectacle, but now he had recovered and ran off into the dunes, hot on the heels of his mark. I grabbed Dad as I ran past and together with Tilly we followed right behind, up and over the dunes, then onto the beach where we spied Anxious lit up by the searchlight, the helicopter low and angled with its front down as it circled my best buddy and the person he would now never let get away.

People came running from all directions. Tony with his friend who'd both been questioned by the police, the owners, some of the others from the bar, and the guy who manned the exit. Phil, Gummo, and Shorty, the ex-army buddies, were grouped together and Phil was shouting into a radio then pointing as he looked at the helicopter. This must have been down to them, as who else could call up a buddy and get a helicopter here?

Everyone was converging on the person furthest away; there was no way they could escape now. They'd taken their chance and blown it, and now there was nothing they could do but give up and hope Anxious left their ankles intact.

But they seemed to have other ideas, and rather than stop, they kept running back and forth along the beach, trying to get back up to the dunes but failing as every time they got close the helicopter would race ahead, turn, then angle the nose down so the blades whipped up sand and were so close to the ground they could probably take your head off.

Our mark raced back down the beach then spun sharply and stood stock still and lifted the rifle. Not to the helicopter, but to me and Dad, and we dropped like stones to the sand as a silent bullet whizzed past us. This had to end, and it had to end now, and I thought it had as Shorty barrelled in from the side and knocked the assassin to the ground. Not to be outdone, the killer slammed the rifle into his head and ran off in a panic, with Shorty gripping the rifle by the barrel.

The helicopter circled, the search light trained on them, and we closed in. Anxious was having a blast, barking and spinning in circles. Working himself into a frenzy, he tore off ahead.

Chapter 19

"Min, what are you doing here?" I shouted, ducking down as I raced towards her, my hair whipping into my face as the downdraft from the helicopter blades grew so fierce I worried I'd be pushed into the ground.

"What?" she hollered, crouching low, hands cupped to her mouth, her blond locks swirling in the maelstrom.

I reached her, wrapped my arms around her, and said, "It's so good to see you, but why did you come? Why didn't you call?"

"Because I knew you'd say everything was fine. Jack phoned and told me what happened. You kept getting kidnapped from me! Max, I thought we promised no secrets?" Min looked up into my eyes, hers full of tears, and then she hugged me tight.

"I'm sorry," I whispered into her hair, her familiar scent almost overwhelming me. It was so good to see her I could hardly breathe. "I didn't want to worry you, and I know you're so busy with work."

"I quit!"

I pulled away and held her at arm's length. "You did?" I couldn't help grinning.

"Yes, but don't look so happy about it. I couldn't go on the way I have been. So stressed, always busy, you always away having all these adventures."

"So, what does that mean?"

"It means I have time to myself to think about things."

"Oh." I was hoping she'd say something else, but I understood. "We need to finish this. It's dangerous. You should go."

"I'm going nowhere. What's happening? Looks like you're busy." Min smirked as the chaos grew more intense.

"Yeah, kinda. We have to get our murderer. The one in the balaclava."

"Oh, right, why didn't you say so?" Anxious came tearing back and jumped into Min's arms and received the adoration he was due, but Min only took a moment to make a fuss of him then let him down.

"Max, what are you doing?" gasped Tilly as she ran past after the group chasing the killer.

"Just saying hello to the love of my life. Sorry, Min, but I have to go. Anxious, go catch our killer."

"Hello," Tilly shouted over her shoulder as she tried to catch up with Anxious who was already closing on the others.

I nodded to Min, then with her by my side we sprinted up the beach where the entire group was now circling the panicked assassin. The helicopter bobbed above us, the spotlight fixed on the killer, then Phil's radio crackled. He said something into it, and the helicopter rose, the light went out, and it flew off, kicking up sand from the dunes.

The peace that filled the roar was so intense it felt like I'd lost my hearing, but the chatter from the others soon filled the void.

My folks jogged up to us and in typical Mum style she said, "Ooh, Min, you alright, love? Great to see you."

"Any problems with the drive?" asked Dad, combing his hair back.

"Um, no. Came straight here. Thanks for calling me. And thanks for letting me know where you were. This place is massive."

"Give us a hug," insisted Mum, and grabbed Min before she had the chance to protest.

"Guys, can this wait, please? In case you've forgotten, we have to deal with something more important."

"Nothing is more important than family, Max," tutted Dad with a shake of his head.

"Absolutely," agreed Mum happily.

"It is lovely to see you all," said Min, glancing at me to see what we should do next.

"You murdered Ben and Russell," screeched Tilly, and lunged forward.

"Easy," I warned, and dragged her back before she went too wild.

"He did it. Owen murdered them, Max." She spun to the masked figure and accused, "Owen, you killed our friends. Your friends. How could you?"

The figure remained silent, head turning left to right, searching for a way out of this. There was no escape, with us, the army buddies, Tony, and others from the bar and restaurant, and Tilly, who I suspected was capable of taking this foul creature down single-handed.

"Tilly, it isn't Owen," I said softly, trying to calm her. "Thank you for coming, everyone, and for helping to catch our murderer. I'm sorry I couldn't let you in on the plan properly, but I knew they'd come for me first before I told everyone who the killer was, and I was right. They tried to shoot me, but we chased them off, and I have to say, Phil, that the helicopter was a surprise, but at least now there's proof of who killed your friends. They tried to assassinate me, and I bet they used the same weapon that they did to shoot the others. But it's not Owen."

"Then who is it?" asked Phil, wiping sweat from his brow.

Everyone closed in on the panicked figure, but they knew the game was up and there was nowhere to go now. They were trapped; no way could they escape without the rifle.

I stepped forward and gave a word to Anxious who sat in front of the person and growled a warning. As they looked down, distracted, I whipped my hand out and snatched the balaclava from their head.

"It's Willow," I said rather needlessly, as everyone could see who it was.

"Who's that, love?" asked Mum merrily. I got the suspicion she and Dad had been imbibing too many glasses of wine while they waited for the action.

"It's that Owen's wife," explained Dad. "From up at the farm."

"Oh, right. Um, why is it her? This makes no sense."

"Willow, how could you?" asked Tilly, shocked to discover that what I'd told her was right, and it wasn't Owen at all.

"She's a woman," said Shorty.

"Well done, Sherlock," laughed Phil, slapping him on the back.

"I don't get it," admitted Gummo.

"I don't think any of us do," said Tony, scratching his head, looking confused. "Are we saying Willow here murdered Ben, hid him under the van, then killed Russell, too, and tried to kill Max? Why on earth would she do that?"

"Maybe we should ask her?" I suggested.

Numerous torches were focused on Willow as she squirmed under the attention. Her camouflage clothes made her look sinister as she scowled at everyone then focused her attention on me. "You tricked me?"

"I did. I knew you'd try to stop me before I revealed everything to the others, and getting Tilly to tell everyone that I had proof was sure to get back to you. I assume Owen told you what he'd heard here, and you decided to come and make sure I didn't tell anyone? Anxious got your scent off the handkerchief you gave me, so I knew it was you."

"What else could I do? I had to try and stop you. Now it's ruined. You make me sick. All of you. So dumb. I drove in and out without a care in the world and you never even knew. Neither did Owen. We're always sharing the quad, so he had no idea what I'd done, so don't you dare try to blame him."

"But why?" asked Tilly.

"You wouldn't understand. None of you would."

"Is he family? Did he do something so bad you had to kill Ben? Was Russell involved too?" Tilly bunched her fists, her face red and angry, but she held it together and didn't attack, just seemed to deflate and her shoulders sagged.

"I bet she's a daughter of that Ben," piped up Mum, looking smug.

"She's too old," said Dad. He turned and added, "No offence."

"Is that it?" asked Tilly. "You shot our friends, your friends, because he's your father? No, that can't be right. Is he Owen's father?"

"Don't be so stupid," spat Willow. "He was a child when I was born, and Owen knows who his parents are. Oh, it's no use! I can't do this any longer. Forgive me? Please forgive me. I don't know what I've done, not really. What that horrid, mean man did was too much. It made me see red. I had one way to find peace in this life and he ruined it, broke it, and didn't even care. Just shrugged his shoulders and said it didn't matter. Well, it did matter, and he knew it!" A broken woman, Willow slumped and sat on the sand, her hands over her face.

Nobody spoke as they tried to take in what she'd said, that this seemingly nice woman had murdered two men and tried to kill me.

I stepped forward and squatted in front of Willow, then waited until she looked up. "Can you explain? Why did you do it? Was it the tree?"

Willow's head shot up. "How did you know?"

I shrugged. "What you just said. That it was your quiet place, where you feel safe and calm and free. An oasis amidst the chaos. What happened? Did Ben damage the tree and it had to be cut down?"

"He was supposed to look after my garden! He'd been coming for years, helping me get it exactly right. Pruning, mowing, tending to the moss, caring for everything. He was always an odd man, never spoke much and always lied when he did, but we got on and he did the work without a fuss. He had an eye, a real feel for how things should be and what felt balanced. Truly in tune with nature."

"So he made a decision you didn't agree with?"

"It was the first tree I ever planted. The day Owen and I got married and we moved into the farmhouse. It was chaos, stuff everywhere, but out in the back garden I saw a way to have my own slice of paradise, so I went out that very day and bought a young acer and cleared away some junk and dug a hole and planted it with Ben's help. I was so proud of myself and had all these ideas for what I'd do. Ben used to stay at the farm even back then and I told him what I wanted, and he had some incredible ideas. He helped me when Owen was too busy or I was too tired and slowly the garden became what it is today. Then he chopped down my tree! He cut it down with a saw like it meant nothing. Said it had to go as it was spoiling the flow of the garden. I didn't care! It was my tree. Mine!" Willow sobbed into her hands, hiding her face, broken, lost to a madness none of us could ever understand.

"It's alright," I said, reaching out and lifting her head. "Tell us the rest. You owe everyone that much. What happened next?"

Willow recovered enough to wipe her eyes, then reached out to me. I helped her to stand then stepped away, not trusting she wouldn't do something we'd both regret, but I could see in her eyes that she was beaten and was going nowhere. She wanted this to be over. She needed to explain. If for no other reason than to try to get us to understand. She was clearly unwell; something inside her had snapped.

"He said the tree was wrong, and that it was too large and the limbs ruined the rest of the space. When I entered the garden, I saw red and we had a huge fight. He stormed off and I vowed I'd get my revenge. The next day, Owen was out on the farm somewhere and said he'd be gone all day, so I took the quad and came here and found Ben. But you were there, too, Max, but I couldn't wait so I hit you. Then I marched Ben back to his stupid van and shot him. I knew it was a risk taking the body away in the daytime, so hid him under the van and planned on getting him later. But Russell saw me, and I chased after him. He was afraid, and would have gone to the police, but I offered him money. He practically bit my hand off at the offer of a few thousand pounds and when we met at the time arranged, I just shot him too. It seemed like the easiest option."

"You locked Anxious in a cupboard," I reminded her. "Why?"

"Because he wouldn't stop barking and he was whining over your body and I panicked. I'm sorry. I love animals and would never do anything so cruel, but I think I've lost my mind. I was surprised he didn't pick up on my scent when you came to the house, but then I remembered that I'd put on Owen's clothes, so it must have confused him. They always stink of cows. I still can't believe this is real. Is it? Am I having a bad dream? Did I really do these terrible things because of a tree?"

"No, not because of a tree," I soothed. "Because it was your only escape from what surrounded you. The chaos. The sheer volume of things. It was your special place."

"It was!" wailed Willow. "My only chance to be happy. To be still and enjoy life. I don't mind the hoarding. I know it's part of me and Owen. It's how we are and I wouldn't change any of it no matter what anyone says. But then Ben cut down my tree. My tree! It meant so much, it held so many memories, and he got rid of it like it was a weed. He's the monster, not me!"

"I think we've heard enough," said Phil.

Dad grabbed his arm as Phil moved towards Willow with Shorty and Gummo beside him and they paused.

"You got something to say?" growled Phil, shaking Dad off.

"Let the lady talk. She's clearly not well and needs to speak. To explain properly."

"She already explained."

"Not everything. What's the matter, Willow? How did it come to this? Have you had issues in the past?"

"What?" Willow glanced over at Dad and the ex-soldiers like she was seeing them for the first time. I don't think she even really knew what was happening or who was here, everyone surrounding her in little pools of light cast by our torches. She looked like a little lost child, not a murderer.

"Tell us everything," said Mum. "What happened to you? Have you been seeing a doctor?"

"A doctor? Yes, yes I have. Things have been getting too much for me. I take tablets. But they don't seem to agree with me and sometimes I go a bit funny. My Owen looks out for me though. He's such a darling and I don't deserve him. But I'm not a violent person. I would never... could never... Oh, what have I done?"

I had a word with Tilly and she and the others left to return to their homes or lodgings, and she said she'd call the police. Phil and the guys had calmed down now the adrenaline had dissipated, and we kept a close eye on Willow as Mum and Min helped her to walk off the beach and up to our pitch. We sat the broken woman in a chair and I made coffee for everyone, and let Willow talk it out, knowing this was her last night of freedom. She wasn't a bad person, or not just a bad person.

As I'd grown to learn since my travels began, sometimes things weren't as simple as they seemed. Yes, what'd happened was awful, but what sane person would do such things? Sometimes the killer knew exactly what they were doing and had no remorse, but usually it was much more complicated than that and they had issues nobody could understand. What may seem inconsequential to those on the outside was the complete opposite to them, and somewhere deep inside a connection went wonky and they did unspeakable things. It didn't justify it, but it never made for an outcome you rejoiced over. Two men were still dead, a woman was broken so badly she killed because her little oasis where she could find peace and a way to cope with the madness that raged around her had been taken away. She'd simply snapped.

The police arrived soon enough and took Willow away. She didn't protest, and just before she got into the police car she turned and looked into my eyes.

"Thank you, Max. Thank you so much."

"What for?" I asked, puzzled.

"For understanding. For not judging me too harshly. I know it was wrong, but life feels like a dream." She smiled as her eyes flashed in the pulse of the red and blue lights from the police car, and in that instant I saw the true extent of her madness and shuddered.

Mum and Dad stayed for a glass of wine, then left. Both were exhausted and wanted to get to bed.

Min and I sat and drank another glass while I went through the whole story with her, unsurprised to learn that Dad had called Min after I'd been kidnapped and told her what happened. She'd come as soon as she was able, and scolded me for not telling her. I apologised, but explained that I didn't want to worry her.

"Don't you get it?"

"Get what?" I asked.

"I want to worry. I want to be part of things. I need to be in your life."

We slept in Vee, squashed as usual as Anxious stole more of the bed than he left for us, but who cared? Min was here, and that meant for a very peaceful night's sleep.

Chapter 20

"Morning." Min yawned from the step to Vee and stretched her arms overhead, looking like a goddess as the orange sun caught her hair and lit her up in a glorious glow.

"Morning. Wow, you look beautiful. Did you sleep alright?"

"I did. And thank you for the compliment. Was that real last night? It seems like it was a dream, as Willow said."

"Maybe we're all caught up in a dream of some kind. Yes, it was real, but in a way I wish it wasn't."

"I know. The poor woman. What a thing to do over a tree."

"Sometimes it's the little things that tip people over the edge. It had clearly been building for years, and it just took the tree being chopped down for her to lose her grip on reality. She'll get the help she needs."

"You solved another case. My hero." Min stepped down and came over to me then kissed my cheek, beaming at me.

"I don't know about hero, but I'm glad it's over. It got quite scary at times, but Anxious was so brave and I couldn't have done it without him."

"He is wonderful, isn't he? Max, Jack told me what happened when Ben's buddies took you both. That you told them not to hurt Anxious and to let him go, but do what they had to with you. That was so selfless."

"I knew you'd never forgive me if anything happened to him." I laughed, and squeezed Min's hand.

"I can't imagine life without either of you. Now, where's my coffee?"

"So sorry for the delay," I teased, then poured us both a cup.

Min nipped off to use the bathroom while I woke Anxious and set the rock n roll bed back to the bench seat position, then he said hello to Min when she returned before racing off to use the dogs' loos, which were much larger and a lot more accessible.

After coffee, Min insisted I take Anxious for a short walk while she got ready for the day, as she said she would stay over if that was alright, and we could have a nice day together.

So it was with a spring in our step that we went for a walk, enjoying the early morning sunshine, happy despite recent events, and looking forward to a day hanging out with Min and my folks.

I wondered how Willow was faring, and hoped she wasn't too scared and wasn't in too much mental anguish, but I doubted that was the case at all. The moment I'd spoken to Tilly about the quad coming and going it had clicked into place that it was most likely Willow, not Owen who had killed the men, but I couldn't quite put my finger on why I suspected her at first until I recalled something he'd said.

He was short-sighted and needed glasses to see any distance. At their house, he'd put them on when we were in the garden as Willow pointed out the collared doves at the far end. The killer hadn't worn glasses. Strange that I hadn't made the connection and suspected Willow, but that's the wiring of the human brain for you. You might not be consciously aware of what was going on in your head, but it knew things even if you weren't aware.

And right now I had that tingling at the base of my neck and knew that something was going on.

I called for Anxious and we hurried back up the

beach, the scene of the madness last night, then took the path through the dunes and marched back to the pitch. I prayed Min was alright, although something assured me she was, but that there was also something very important going on.

Not knowing why, Anxious and I nevertheless slowed as we got close and he began to belly crawl while I crouched over, scanning for danger, ears primed for the slightest noise. Min was nowhere to be seen, but as we approached Vee I heard a strange hissing noise, then a rattle like somebody was shaking a…

"The graffiti vandal!" I shouted, and shot upright, then raced around the gazebo to the driver's side of Vee, ready to nab the person who had been intermittently spraying peculiar artwork on my home for months now.

Anxious barked as he took the shortcut underneath Vee and emerged just as I got around the van.

Min stood there, spray can in hand, smiling at us and not looking the least bit guilty.

"You caught me," she giggled, then bent and with a flourish sprayed a perfect curve in black, outlining the purple and white of what had been a half-finished symbol or maybe a letter.

"Min, what on earth are you doing? Was it you all along?"

"It was!" she said proudly, straightening, then dropping the can. "And it was one mystery you never solved. Ha!"

"Why would you do this? What does it mean? You've been spraying the van little by little each time you stayed over?"

"I have. Bit by bit early in the morning or late at night, and you never guessed it was me. But now it's done."

"It is?"

"Yes, come here. Come and take a look."

Anxious and I shrugged at each other, then joined Min and stood back to admire her artwork.

"Read it," she insisted, smiling, her cheeks flushed with excitement.

"What on earth is going on? Why have you been doing this? I don't understand."

"Just read it, you silly fool." Min reached out and took my hand, then turned me to face the van.

I studied the stylised writing, and gradually began to make out the words. "Will you?" I read. Turning to Min, I admitted, "I don't get it."

"Seriously?" Min frowned, her eyes dancing with excitement, and began hopping from one foot to the other. "Then you better read the rest. Come around to the other side." Min led me back to the gazebo. Anxious ducked under the van again and emerged beside us.

I stared at the finished art and slowly the seemingly abstract marks began to make sense. "Is that an M?"

"Yes, of course it is. Read the rest!"

I stared at the finished art and read two words that will forever bring me joy. "Marry me?" I read slowly, finally understanding what the half-finished swirls had been leading up to. Now it was done, it became clear what her intentions had been all along.

"Well?" she asked.

"You mean it?"

"Of course I do. I'm sorry I took so long to finish it, but it's really hard to use those cans and I even had to get lessons so I wouldn't mess it up. Now it's done. So, what do you think?" Min took my other hand in hers, and looked into my eyes. "Max Effort, will you marry me?"

"Yes! Of course! What about living in Vee? What about toilets and showers and Anxious nicking all the bed?"

The little guy whined, then pouted, but he knew something great was happening and barked for joy.

"Yes, Anxious," said Min, "we're going to be a real family again. We're going to live together and have adventures and walks every morning and it will be wonderful."

"You're sure?" I asked, feeling lightheaded and on top of the world. "Really?"

"Yes, really. I know I should have agreed for us to be together again months ago, but I had to be sure. We both did."

"Min, this is awesome. I can't believe it was you all along."

"I know it was naughty, but once I got the idea I couldn't stop myself. So, what's it to be? A big wedding in a church, the registry office, or something else?"

"How about at a cool campsite somewhere?"

"That's what I was going to say. It will be perfect. Just us, your parents, close friends, and our best man."

We turned to Anxious, who did a double take and looked behind him, then slowly turned back to us, eyes wide.

"Yes, you're the best man, Anxious. If you agree?"

A bark in the affirmative meant the agreement was made.

I kissed Min and spun her around, happier than I'd ever been in my life.

"Then let's get married!" whooped Min.

"Right away," I agreed.

"And let's just this once not get embroiled in any drama." Min's eyes flashed with mischief.

We both laughed and laughed, as what could possibly happen that could spoil our future together?

The End

Except it isn't. Read on for a delicious one-pot wonder, then be sure to read my little note afterwards. Will Max and Min really get to tie the knot and live happily ever after, or will something get in their way? They've been through so much together, but I think we know the gang well enough by now to know that there's just the slightest chance that whatever Min says, they might get embroiled in another murder mystery before the end of the series. Get ready for the last book!

Recipe

Burrito Delight

I have a terrible admission to make, and please don't hold it against me. For many years, we made burritos completely wrong. Too wet, no rice, too many options, and absolutely not the right tortillas. Now we have it down to a fine art, and it's time to share. Of course, as Max said, there are no end of recipes, and that's the beauty of a great burrito. Choose your meat, your spices, your heat level, your salad bits, even your tortillas, but if you only take one piece of advice, it's get the absolute best ones you can. Surprisingly, we find that an Italian variety known as Crosta & Mollica Piadina are perfect for the job, take heat well, and don't go flaky or disintegrate like some other brands. But try a few and see what works for you, of course.

Ingredients

For the chicken:

- Boneless chicken thighs - 4
- Smoked paprika - 1 tbsp
- Ground cumin - 1/2 tbsp
- Olive oil - 2 tbsp

For the rice:

- Garlic - 3 cloves crushed
- Fresh coriander - 1 bunch, stems chopped finely, leaves chopped roughly
- Borlotti beans - 1 tin, rinsed and drained

- Leftover basmati rice - 200g
- Juice and zest of one lime

For the slaw:

- White cabbage - 1/4 grated
- Apple - 1 grated
- Spring onions - 3 finely chopped
- Red chilli - 1 deseeded and very finely chopped
- Greek yogurt - 2 tbsp
- Juice of one lemon

To serve:

- Good flavourful cheddar - 100g grated
- Good quality large wraps

Method

- First off bash the chicken thighs with a heavy rolling pin between two sheets of grease proof paper until they're around 1/2cm thick. In a bowl, mix with the spices, a little salt and pepper along with half the olive oil.
- Heat a heavy frying pan on a medium high heat and cook the chicken for around ten minutes until well charred on the outside, moist and cooked through on the inside. You know the deal, no pink juices!
- While that's going on, warm the rest of the oil in a pan and gently heat the garlic and coriander stems. Once things are fragrant add the beans, rice, and lime (juice and zest). Once its properly heated

- through, stir in the rest of the coriander - pop a lid on and turn off the heat.
- Really you should be making a salsa, maybe some avocado or other salad. We're keeping this simple, and more van friendly. Mix all the slaw ingredients together. Done!
- To serve, warm through each wrap, top with rice, slaw, chicken, and cheese, then fold up and enjoy!

These began as Jamie's simple burritos, and then became Max's and ours. Make them yours with more spice, salsa, different beans, other meat. But don't make them too wet and do get good wraps. Perfect travelling food.

Disfruta!

From the Author

I think we can all agree that Max and Min deserve a happy future together, but who saw that coming? It was Min all along who was spray-painting Vee, but I don't think Max holds it against her.

The final book in the series now awaits, so be sure to check out Resolutions and Executions and follow them on their last adventure before their lives change for good. It's going to be a wild one, that much I can tell you, but there's no doubt they were made for each other and I can't wait to see what's next for them. Maybe we'll find out, but to know what I'm hinting at here you'll have to read to the very end of the next book of Max's Campervan Case Files.

Get ready because here we go…

Be sure to stay updated about new releases and fan sales. You'll hear about them first. No spam, just book updates at www.authortylerrhodes.com.

You can also follow me on Amazon www.amazon.com/stores/author/B0BN6T2VQ5.

Connect with me on Facebook www.facebook.com/authortylerrhodes/.

Printed in Dunstable, United Kingdom